An Island Christmas Reader

An Island Christmas Reader

DAVID WEALE

with illustrations by
Dale McNevin
&
Joey Weale

Charlottetown
1994

"The Christmas Orange" and "The Christmas Concert" previously appeared in *Them Times* (Institute of Island Studies, Charlottetown, 1992).
Book design by Julie Scriver, Goose Lane Editions.
Printed and bound in Canada by Williams & Crue, Ltd., Summerside.

10 9 8 7 6 5 4 3 2

Canadian Cataloguing in Publication Data

Weale, David, 1942
   An Island Christmas reader
   ISBN 0-9698606-0-9

1. Christmas — Prince Edward Island.   I. Title.
GT4987.15.W52 1994   394.2'663'09717   C94-950223-5

Published by
The Acorn Press
P.O. Box 22024
Charlottetown, Prince Edward Island
CANADA C1A 9J2

Distributed by
Tangle Layne Distribution
P.O. Box 3086
Charlottetown, Prince Edward Island
CANADA C1A 7P1

To my children, and the memory of their Christmas wonder

Contents

Acknowledgements

I am grateful to all those Islanders who contributed to the writing of this book by sharing with me their stories and memories of Christmas. I recall fondly conversations in many kitchens, the innumerable cups of tea and coffee, and the occasional splash of rum, which we enjoyed during our discussions.

I would also like to thank my students at the University of Prince Edward Island for the information they gathered in their oral history assignments over the past few years.

Finally, my thanks to Catherine Hennessey, who first suggested a book of Christmas essays; to Russell Downe, who shared with me the stories of Charlie Chamberlain and the woman from Bear River; to Dale McNevin and my son Joe, for enhancing the stories with their wonderful illustrations; to Laurie Brinklow, my editor and publisher, for her encouragement and good judgement; and to Evelyn McMurrer, my typist, for her patient and good-natured electronic midwifery during the long nativity.

December

There is a wisdom in December —
relaxed,
unbuttoned,
expended and slumberous,
the land falls back into itself.

A pale lemon brightness
in the grey flannel sky,
and a shining watchful crow,
high on a bare branch:
his impertinent majesty,
presiding over the winter landscape
like a Lord.

December 1990

Christmas, 1775:
Salt Fish and Potatoes and Thankful For It

One of the earliest recorded references to Christmas on Prince Edward Island is also one of the most dismal. It appears in the journal of Thomas Curtis, a young sawyer from Hampshire, England, who was shipwrecked on one of the long sandspits off the North Shore, near Cascumpec, in early November, 1775. The saga of the passengers and crew of the *Elizabeth* is one of the most tragic and sorrow-stricken accounts from that rude colonial period.

Like many other emigrants at the time, Curtis embarked for the New World with high hopes for improving his station in life. His sponsor, Robert Clark, the proprietor of Lot 21, had led him to believe that a veritable paradise awaited him on Prince Edward Island. In this he was to be bitterly disappointed. It was not a paradise he discovered, but a frozen hell, and his account of the months following the wreck is the story of a desperate, life-and-death struggle to survive the harsh Island winter.

Curtis, along with the other men, women and children, spent ten harrowing days on the exposed off-shore sandhill, as marooned and immobilized as their grounded vessel. They looked on helplessly as breaker after breaker crashed against the side of the wrecked *Elizabeth*, and as they watched the terrible buffeting, they experienced the foundering of their cherished hopes for a better life. When the small lifeboat which had gone off for help returned they were able at last to make their way to the originally intended destination of New London, some forty-six miles to the east. Ragged, sodden and half-starved, their condition was so much altered by the rigours of their ordeal that, according to Curtis, they "hardly knew one another at a little distance." It was, therefore, with glad anticipation that they approached the settlement.

When they came in sight of the place, their spirits were shattered by the droll scene which awaited them. The settlement was nothing more than a random collection of sixteen small cabins, not one of which, according to Curtis, was any better than a "Cow house." "This," he wrote sarcastically, "comprised the whole of the famous New London."

He confessed that the sight of the community was so altogether different from the idea he had formed of it that he immediately repented of his voyage, and began to wish himself in "Olde London" again; and, as the remorseless cold of the Island winter encroached, he was filled with serious doubt about whether or not he and the others could survive until spring. Like many other early settlers he occupied his mind with the thought of how he might one day escape the cursed spot in which he had landed.

Curtis made arrangements to winter with a Compton family. Their crude, drafty dwelling was so low in places it was impossible for him to stand upright, and while it provided some shelter from the punitive wind, there were many nights when the cold was so severe he was unable to sleep. One morning when he arose he observed a scene which attested graphically to the frigidity of the temperature inside the house. Joseph Rooke, another man who was sharing the same quarters, was asleep in his bed. Curtis observed that during the night the condensation from Rooke's breath had formed a large icicle which extended from his mouth and down his chest some sixteen to eighteen inches. It was approximately four inches wide and two inches thick near his mouth. "This," commented Curtis wryly, "convinced me that this Island would not be agreeable to an English constitution."

The only food the Comptons had to offer was salt fish and potatoes. Curtis noted that this diet was not altogether disagreeable, and that most days he was able to eat it with a "tolerable good appetite." He also noted, with his characteristically sardonic humour, that in order to introduce some variety into the diet they would sometimes eat the food hot, and other times cold.

During the day most of their time was spent in the forest, cutting wood for the greedy fire, and hauling it home on a sledge. Curtis obviously hated the winter woods where, he claimed, "the snow is ten or twelve feet deep on a level. . . . " He noted it was especially hazardous to walk over trees that had blown down and been covered over with snow. Often, he lamented, it was not possible to detect them, "till you tred on them and sink in far over head and Ears."

At Christmastime of that year Curtis and a couple of other men made an excursion three or four miles along the shore to visit a small mill operated by an "American." The man invited them into his home and Curtis recorded that his heart ached when he observed the distressed conditions of the household. The miller had a wife and "eight or nine" small children, the oldest being not more than ten years. The man apologized that he could give them no food, informing them that he had but a small stock of provisions to last through the winter. He then shared with them what must go down in Island history as the most simple Christmas treat of all time — a drink of water.

Curtis and the men then returned to New London to a Christmas repast of salt fish and potatoes, which, he said, he "relished well"; further, it is difficult not to be moved by his final observation on the day. In the spirit of a true survivor he remarked bravely that he was "happy" he was "no worse off." It is difficult to imagine how much worse off he could have been.

There are no descendants of Thomas Curtis on the Island today. Early the next spring, in May, 1776, he boarded a brig in Malpeque Harbour and happily departed Prince Edward Island. Before he left he took one parting swipe at the place where he had endured so much. "I may now say," he wrote, "I have been on this well recommended Island abought six months and have not seen the Colour of the land."

Nine months later Curtis arrived back in England, and concluded his journal with a burst of thanksgiving. "I can't," he wrote, "express the Joy I felt when I got on my native Country the 2nd of February 1777." We hear no more of him after that, but it is possible to imagine that for the rest of his life he told the story of the wild place he had visited: a place so hard and impoverished he was thankful for a Christmas libation of clear, cold water, and a Christmas dinner of salt fish and potatoes.

DECORATIONS

"Red Rose tea came packed in aluminum foil paper. The paper stuck
to this foil was removed gently with hot water, then the foil was pressed
out carefully by hand, and placed in a special box. By Christmas there might
be two dozen sheets of foil. Sometimes we would take this foil from the
bulk tea and place it on the top of the broom handle to form the shape
of a bell. Then we would shove a needle through the end so we could
hang them on the tree."

Montague

"Spruce cones were collected and dipped in soap suds and left to harden,
leaving a pretty white covering over the dull brown colour."

Kinkora

"My grandmother's favourite Christmas decorations were the
little metal birds that held the candles in place on the tree.
They were painted bright colours. The spring in the tail was how
you attached them to the tree."

Murray Harbour

"The tree was decorated with teafoil tinsel. Betty recalls how
pretty it was in the daylight. The woodstove caused the air to
circulate and she can remember the tinsel twinkling
and being so pretty."

O'Leary

The Eaton's Beauty

When I walked into the room I noticed her immediately. Dressed in a crimson velvet dress, she was seated regally in a white wicker chair, her long dark hair falling over her shoulders, front and back. She was beautiful, with large serene brown eyes and a captivating smile on her smallish mouth. I also noticed that she wasn't wearing any shoes. When my host, who was standing next to me, saw me staring with such apparent interest she asked if I would like to hold her. "I certainly would," I replied, and walked over and picked her up.

"She's over seventy years old," she informed me — and with that the story began.

When Ella Chappell, née Thompson, of York was a little girl growing up in North River, she and her sister Olive each received from an invalid aunt a Christmas present which was so far beyond their expectations they could scarcely believe their good fortune. Like many other girls at that time they had spent hours poring over the toy section of the Eaton's catalogue. "It was our prayer book," was how Ella put it. And of all the wonderful items they perused in that catalogue there was none more alluring than "the Eaton's Beauty," a doll attired in a fancy lace-frilled dress with a wide ribbon which ran diagonally across her front. She had moveable joints, and eyes with long lashes which opened magically when she was picked up, and closed when she was laid down.

But "the Eaton's Beauty" cost $1.98, an amount equivalent to several days wages in that farming society of the 1920s. Being members of a large family, it was utterly unthinkable that they might ever actually receive such an extravagant present, and so they imagined, but dared not hope; dreamed, but dared not wish.

Another woman from that same generation told me that she always wanted an Eaton's Beauty but never got one. One year, instead of giving her what she wanted her mother re-dressed an old doll in new clothes. "I was not impressed," she added ruefully. Ella and Olive Thompson were more fortunate, and on that memorable Christmas over seventy years ago, the unthinkable happened. When the wrapping came off the presents there were two dolls, one for each of them. "My soul, we were excited," exclaimed Ella, "because $1.98 then would be like $200.00 today. At that time, you know eggs were ten cents a dozen, and a yeast cake was four cents."

The two dolls were almost identical. The only difference between them was that one had brown eyes — like Ella — and the other blue — like Olive. It seemed a perfect coincidence.

The little girls named their dolls — both of them — after their Aunt Lizzie, the patroness responsible for their good fortune. Olive got her word in first and named her doll Elizabeth Mary. Ella, with a stroke of childish ingenuity, settled for Mary Elizabeth. And in talking with Ella I got the clear impression that, in this ritual of naming, the two girls, the two dolls, and their beloved aunt were joined together in a pact of indissoluble affection which has remained, undiminished, over the years. "I always thought so much of my aunt," added Ella, "that when I gave birth to my only daughter she was called Elizabeth Ann — after Aunt Lizzie."

When the girls were older, and the dolls began to show the wear and tear of being present at so many tea parties, and of having their hair combed so often, their mother placed them in a trunk where they remained for over thirty years. They might have stayed there even longer if it had not been for a trip Ella took to Toronto to visit Olive who had married and moved there years before. "I saw this sign up on a store, *Doll Hospital*," recalled Ella,

"and I thought about those dolls in the trunk. I said to Olive, 'I think we'd better send the dolls up to the hospital and get their eyes fixed, and get new wigs.'"

And that's exactly what they did. The $1.98 dolls each received a $100.00 treatment which restored them to their original condition. "I was so excited," said Ella, "I was just in my second childhood when my sister came back from Toronto and brought those dolls."

A few years later Ella was shopping at Norton's in Charlottetown, and spied a small, white wicker chair, with a teddy bear seated in it. Immediately she thought of her doll. She asked the clerk if the chair was for sale and was informed that it was. The price was $65.00. "My word," she thought, "I'd hardly pay $65.00 for my own chair, but if it's for the doll then that's all right." She took out her purse and paid the money, and now the doll sits in that very chair, in her living room in York, a daily reminder of dear Aunt Lizzie, her sister Olive, and her own Christmas bliss of long ago.

And so I picked up the doll, and was surprised by the amazement I felt when those big brown eyes opened wide. I tilted her back and lifted her up several times, just for the pleasure of it, and caught myself smiling back.

DECORATIONS

"My grandparents' house was beautiful that Christmas. It smelled like cinnamon and oranges. There was a beautiful Christmas tree with store-bought decorations that were made in Germany. They were so detailed and colourful I looked at them for hours. I didn't even know where Germany was."

O'Leary

"Fancy handkerchiefs were very popular in my time as decorations. We'd take them by the centre and hang them from the branches. They called them hankies in those days. It was before kleenex. And sometimes white handkerchiefs would be starched . . . and folded into fans."

Montague

"We used to save the wood from the match sticks, and then glue coloured paper to the end to make fake flowers out of them."

Miscouche

"They would get to see the tree in all its glory [with the candles lit] only once, for only a few seconds, but it was worth it. The way it was described by Mémé, my grandmother, it must have been absolutely mesmerizing, to stand quietly by as Christmas Day ended with the extinguishing of those candles."

Palmer's Road

"We used to take the red binder twine, and wrap it with ground spruce."

Poplar Point

The Little Christmas Man

The wonder of Christmas was the wonder of things appearing, as if by magic; and, for one Island girl, the magic of an altogether strange person who appeared, and then disappeared, just as unaccountably.

One of the deepest mysteries of creation, a question at the very heart of the universe, is the mystery of how something can come from nothing. But that was exactly what happened every Christmas when I was a child, and I have the distinct recollection of being astounded at the way the gifts on Christmas morning seemed to materialize out of nothing. The gifts themselves were wonderful, and I can remember some of them vividly, but their sudden, overnight appearance was an even deeper wonder.

Unlike children today, most of us never went shopping, and even if we had, there were no toy departments like there are now, where row upon row of selections succeed in so raising the hopes of many children that a measure of disappointment on Christmas morning is almost assured. This relentless, systematic cultivation of expectations, in the stores and on television, was unknown. I don't even recall looking at toys in the catalogue.

Many children, far from being disappointed that they did not receive everything on a long list, were pleased and delighted that they received anything at all. I recognize that this sounds suspiciously like making a virtue out of scarcity, and perhaps it is, but I do know our innocence made it possible to receive very great joy from gifts which today would scarcely be considered worthy of giving. A button on a string; a molasses cookie, or "dough-boy," cut in the shape of a person; a wooden top, fashioned out of a spool with a dowel stuck through the centre hole; a few hard barley animal candies, or "shapes," which you could suck on for days; or a little homemade tap-dancing man made of wood, with hinged knees — these were just a few of the homely, simple gifts which, fifty years ago, were able to evoke joy and gratitude in the hearts of farm children.

One Island woman remembers getting a brown china cup filled with hard candy. That was her only gift that Christmas, but after all these years she thinks of it fondly. Another little girl, from the North Shore, was always wanting to eat the herring roe, but was never permitted.

Then, one Christmas, to her delight, she found a little bottle of it in her stocking. Santa was so knowing!

Children were unlikely to be disappointed with their Christmas presents, for there was little in their experience against which to make a rueful comparison. One Island woman put it this way: "There was one Christmas that I'll never forget. I found in my stocking a grey wool cap. That hat went to bed with me every night, and became my most precious possession. Today, when I picture that cap in my mind, there certainly wasn't anything beautiful about it. But when you never had one to compare it with, it was beautiful indeed."

When I was seven I received from Santa a little tin drum with Buckingham Palace guards in their tall fur hats painted on the side, and a Meccano set, with tiny metal wrenches, and a package of nuts and bolts for holding the parts together. It was a banner year, and I have never forgotten how utterly pleased I was at my good fortune. I had no idea where such things came from. As far as I was concerned I had merely wished for them, and my wishes had somehow resulted in their appearance on Christmas morning. That is the miracle of a child's Christmas: the miracle of the incarnation of wishes.

The visit of Santa was, of course, the logical explanation of this remarkable annual phenomenon, but that only added to the mystery of it all. His appearance, no less than the appearance of the gifts themselves, was something so entirely outside the range of everyday happenings that it inculcated, more deeply perhaps than any other childhood experience, an ineradicable sense of the magical nature of the universe. We were all taught to believe in the goodness of God, but it was the story of Santa that really drove the message home.

I am convinced that our adult commitment to Christmas, and the extravagant effort we invest in the festival year after year, is, more than anything else, our attempt to perpetuate the unsullied wonder of childhood vision. We cling to the memory of a time when the earth, and everything in it, seemed illuminated from within; when a raisin, a nut, or a piece of hard candy were aspects of eternity; when imagination was so powerful there were sleigh-bells in the sky and hoof-beats on the roof; and when, for one Island girl from Miminegash, a late night descent to the parlour brought her face to face with a diminutive Christmas elf.

She was upstairs one Christmas Eve, trying unsuccessfully to go to sleep. Very late she heard a noise downstairs and decided to creep down and see who was there. "When I reached the bottom of the stairs," she recalled, "there was a small, almost leprechaun-like man in the parlour. He was all dressed in red with thin white hair. He was just standing there, so I sat still on the step to watch. But all of a sudden he just disappeared, and to this day I would swear on a stack of Bibles that I did see that miniature man."

I harbour the secret hope every Christmas that, at some gift-wrapped moment during the holiday season, there will be some sight, or sound, or perhaps some smell, that will open up for me the memory of my childhood Christmases. It is the wish that, for just one moment, I might once again be waiting for Santa Claus. There was hope triumphant in that waiting, and a child's faith in the essential goodness of things.

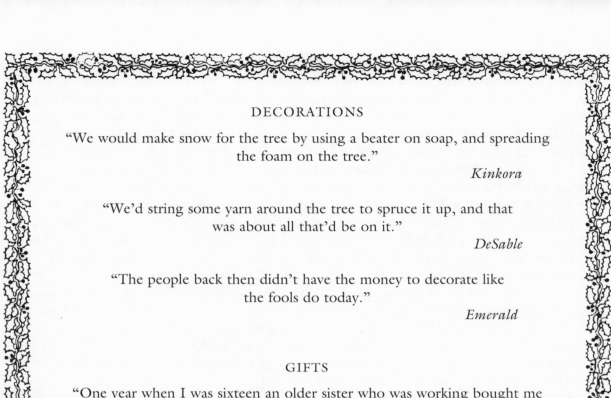

DECORATIONS

"We would make snow for the tree by using a beater on soap, and spreading the foam on the tree."

Kinkora

"We'd string some yarn around the tree to spruce it up, and that was about all that'd be on it."

DeSable

"The people back then didn't have the money to decorate like the fools do today."

Emerald

GIFTS

"One year when I was sixteen an older sister who was working bought me an off-mauve dress, with bloused sleeves and a belt. That was the first piece of clothing I ever had that was store-bought."

St. Peter's

"We each received an orange which was a big thing because they were so hard to come by on the Island in winter. But Grandfather had his connections."

O'Leary

"One year I got a car that was run by batteries, but my parents couldn't afford them. I had to wait till the next Christmas to get them."

Bedford

Chimney Communication

In many homes there was a tradition of sending a note to Santa, not through the mail, but by putting it in the kitchen woodstove. By some kind of special Christmas magic, the message, like smoke in the wind, was carried away to Santa's abode. Evelyn McMurrer who grew up in Argyle Shore remembers very well the time an older sister was attempting, with little success, to convince her sceptical younger siblings of this Christmas miracle. Finally, to prove her point, she took a small piece of paper and lifted the back cover off the stove. When the younger children had gathered round, and all eyes were fixed intently on the spot, she dropped the piece of paper through the hole. The strong draft from the flue immediately wafted the paper up the stovepipe and out of sight. "There!" she exclaimed triumphantly. "Now do you believe me?" They did.

Mary Kells, from East Royalty, told me a story from her childhood which entailed an interesting variation on this common practice. When she was just a little girl, before the first great war, she had a rag doll named Judy, who was very precious to her. One year, shortly before Christmas, Mary came down with scarlet fever and had to be quarantined. All her clothing had to be burned as, unfortunately, did Judy, her cherished doll.

Mary's parents did not, however, tell her that Judy had been incinerated. Hoping to ease the shock of the separation they told her that the doll had flown up the chimney. According to Mary this half-truth left some room for hope. If Judy had flown up the chimney it seemed reasonable to suppose that she, like the Christmas notes, had flown directly to Santa, and that Santa, kind soul that he was, would bring her back on Christmas Eve.

But alas! it was not to be. Christmas came and went, and Mary had to reconcile herself to the fact that Judy's great chimney adventure had been a one-way trip.

Santa, however, did bring another doll.

Another woman shared with me a similar story. When her grandmother, named Tina, was a very young girl, probably around age five, all she wanted for Christmas was a new doll. Her mother told her to write a letter to Santa and then burn it in the woodstove so the request could travel up into the sky with the smoke. She said that when Santa came on Christmas Eve he would know what she wanted because the message would be in the clouds above the house. Tina did what she was told, and as Christmas approached she became more and more excited.

Two days before Christmas the mother awoke to frantic shouting and wailing downstairs. She went down to find her daughter in a state of extreme agitation. Bewildered, the mother asked what was going on. Tina replied with tears in her eyes, "Mom, it's raining out." Her mother, not understanding, replied, "Yes, . . . so?"

"Now Santa won't know what I want for Christmas because the rain is washing away my letter."

Tina's mother had to hide her smile as she told the perturbed little girl not to worry, and that she was certain Santa's helpers had already gotten the message.

Tina awoke on Christmas morning to find her doll. Her faith in Santa, and in the practice of chimney communication, remained intact.

The Boston Box

arly in this century most of the gifts received by children at Christmas came from within the home. They were, for the most part, practical commonplace gifts which, though appreciated, had not the power to evoke the excitement or wonder of a store-bought present. In that rural domain, where most everything was homemade, children might expect to receive a pair of grey mitts or socks knit by grandmother, a rough handsleigh made by father, a doll's dress sewn by mother out of familiar cast-off materials, or a pair of skates, with straps made from old harness, fashioned by the local blacksmith. But they didn't expect anything fancy or extraordinary. Even the fudge was made right there on the kitchen stove, and the ice cream in the back porch.

There was, however, one notable exception to all of this, and that exception was "the Boston box." In some Island homes the arrival of Santa Claus from the North Pole was overshadowed in importance by the arrival of the annual Christmas package from south of the border. If anything novel or bewitching was to find its way under the Christmas tree, it was most liable to come from that source.

Most everyone on Prince Edward Island had relatives in the States; indeed, some children had more aunts and uncles, and more cousins, in Boston than in their home community. What is more, those kin-folk in the United States had jobs that paid regular wages. They worked as carpenters or domestics or street-car conductors, and while most of them certainly weren't rich by big-city standards, in the minds of Islanders they were affluent; and that affluence, however illusory, carried with it an obligation — the obligation of sharing their good fortune with the folks back on the farm. They might have been eight hundred miles away, but that wasn't nearly far enough to escape the long reach of family expectations. And so it was that, at Christmas, many families received in the mail a package from the United States. Most everyone referred to it as "the Boston box," whether it actually came from Boston or not. This was in keeping with the common Island practice of referring to anyone in New England as being in Boston, like the man who is alleged to have told a neighbour that his son was in Boston, "working in the woods."

There was always the chance that there would be things in the Boston box which had never so much as been seen on Prince Edward Island. It was an alluring, wonderful prospect, and the children waited for the package the way anglers wait for April. A woman who grew up in Millview recalled that the big hall window in the upstairs of her house became "a very exciting place" during the weeks before Christmas. She and her brothers and sisters would stand there and wait for the mailman. "Each morning we waited to see if he was going to drop off the big brown parcel from our favourite aunt Mary who lived in Boston. Finally, the morning arrived, and how excited we were as we shouted, 'The parcel is here!' Around the big table in the kitchen we would gather to open it up."

In some homes the arrival of the package from Boston was such an important part of the Christmas celebration that its failure to arrive on time was little short of disastrous. One man from down east told me about the time there was a big storm the week before Christmas which prevented the mail from getting through. "That year," he said, "our parents told us that Santa would be coming at New Year's."

Some older Islanders can remember, even to this day, the gifts they received in the Boston box. A woman, now in her eighties, recalls going to the mailbox the day it arrived and receiving a great fright. When she picked up the box it began to emit strange noises. She was so surprised she dropped the parcel on the ground and ran back up the lane. "I found out later," she said, "that it was a doll that could cry when you picked it up, but I had never heard tell of that." One boy received from Boston a postcard with ten shiny new dimes taped on the back, and another Islander, now an old man, recalls all the cast-off clothes he received. "I can remember thinking that American boys must have awfully long legs," he said, "because the pants I would get in the parcel from the States always fit in the waist, but the legs were too long."

Waiting didn't always end with childhood. One woman, now in her seventies, began getting Christmas gifts from an aunt in Boston when she was a little girl, and received them every year until 1991 when her benefactress became too ill to continue the tradition. It marked the end of an era, not only for the woman, but for the entire province. Oh, there are still Islanders who move away, and packages which arrive at Christmas with postmarks from different provinces and countries, but the annual influx of precious treasures from Boston is now largely a thing of the past. It's too bad, I suppose; but, then again, there were those who weren't altogether unhappy to see the custom come to an end. One woman confessed that she had "mixed feelings" about the parcel from Boston. "It was exciting for the children," she explained, "but it bothered me that they grew up thinking the best things always came from someplace else."

Christmas Tree in the Parlour

February 16, 1993

Dear David Weale,

At Christmas this year I received from my sister on Prince Edward Island a card entitled "Christmas Tree in the Parlour." It featured the same picture which appeared in your book "Them Times." You will perhaps be interested to learn that that picture was taken by me with my little box "Brownie" just after Christmas, 1944. I also thought you might like to know some of the memories and feelings this picture evokes in me.

My husband had gone overseas in the Spring of '44. He flew with the R.A.F. in a crew of mostly R.A.F. boys. The pilot, however, was a Canadian from Ontario. At Christmas of that year they were on leave in London, with "doodle-bugs" flying over at regular intervals — and the boys seeking refuge under the beds in the hotel.

Meanwhile, back on the Island, on December 20, 1944, I gave birth to Barbara Jean, our first child, and we spent Christmas Day in the little hospital on Main Street, Montague. I had gone to Union Road to live with my sister and her husband and children after Alec, my husband, went overseas, and soon after discovered that I was pregnant.

A day or so after Christmas, Barbara and I were transported home in a woodsleigh with a high box. I sat on a bag of bran holding my baby, surrounded by other bags of feed. I was wearing a huge "coon" coat, and we were wrapped in fur "buffaloes" — such comfort! There had been such a snowfall that there were no roads cleared through the countryside, but the big Percheron team took it all in stride, while my brother-in-law guided them through the fields and the wood-road.

The children in the picture are Anna and Billy, my niece and nephew, and their new little cousin. They were very precious to me, especially that Christmas.

My roots are in Cardigan, Kings County, where my father had a small farm in sight of the Cardigan Railway Station. My name was Ruth MacEachern. My husband lived in Cardigan Head and our parents had gone to school together, and to the same church, etc.

Looking back I know we were poor, but we did not know it. We were never told we were poor, nor did we feel poor. By the same token I look at children today and I know that in many ways we were rich — in the things that matter.

With sincere good wishes,
Mrs. Alec MacLeod

P.S. These, of course, were time exposures, hence the grave faces of two very lively children.

GIFTS

"Eric received a pair of factory skates for Christmas from an older sister
in Toronto. None of the children had ever had skates before, only the
homemade ones, and so when Eric saw the skates he was so excited and
happy that he did not know what to do. He skated day and night and
eventually wore the skates until there was no support left in them and he
could not stand up in them any longer. When this happened he switched the
skates and wore them on the opposite feet. That way he got a few more
weeks out of them."

Tyne Valley

"I had seen the little truck in the old variety store down by the run.
It was made of tin, white in colour, and had two small milk bottles in
the back. The bottles were filled with real milk and had tops on them.
I can still remember the feelings I felt when I got up early Christmas
morning and peeked downstairs, but I was caught and sent right back
to bed. Then I got up around 5:00 a.m. and I was feeling even more excited
than I was the first time I got up. And there, before my eyes,
under the tree, was my little white milk truck. I think it was my most
memorable Christmas as a young fella."

Miminegash

"Mildred recalls one Christmas during the Depression. She woke up on
Christmas morning and came bounding down the stairs. In her stocking she
found a dime, that was all. Another year her younger brother set
a big empty box under the tree with the note attached, 'Fill it up Santa.'
His Uncle Lorne came home, took the box to the basement,
and filled it up with potatoes."

Bedeque

The Woman From Bear River

The letter arrived at the Charlottetown Police Station early in January, 1954. The return address was Bear River, and the pencilled handwriting on the front of the envelope could easily have been mistaken for that of a child. It referred to a calamitous chain of events in the life of the sender which had been altered dramatically by the caring intervention of two city policemen. The note recalled a painful episode two weeks earlier when the Christmas spirit had moved unexpectedly to touch the life of a destitute family, where grim poverty had almost succeeded in crushing out the last spark of Christmas cheer.

The dark side of Christmas is the curse of failed expectations, and of sadness, made even more sad, by the contemplation of unhappy circumstances during the season of mandatory joy. That, at least, was how it was for the woman from Bear River. It was the day before Christmas and she was desperate. She had gotten up early that morning, long before daylight, to catch a ride to town on the back of the milk truck. It would be a rough, cold trip, with many stops along the way to pick up the cream cans, standing straight like little armoured sentinels at each farmer's gate; but she was expecting an unemployment cheque, and knew if she didn't go to town to intercept it there would be nothing to put in her children's stockings, and no food for the Christmas table.

The fire had died down during the night and she shivered as she dressed quietly in the darkness of the curtained-off, single-room dwelling which was home to herself and her seven children. Her husband, still in his clothes, had staggered to his bed sometime during the night and would be there when the children woke up. He wouldn't be in any condition to care for them, but she consoled herself with the thought that he would at least be at home, and could be roused in the event of an emergency. She felt guilty about leaving, but the prospect of a Christmas without toys or treats drove her to action. She knew the children would be upset when they discovered her absence, but she had awakened her eleven-year-old daughter, the eldest, and told her of her day's plan. "I will be back by suppertime," she whispered, "so you look after the others, and tell them Santa Claus will be coming tonight." Before leaving the house she removed the cover from the stove, stirred up the few remaining

live coals with the poker, and put in two pieces of wood. It was some comfort to know the chill would be off the room by the time the children got up.

She walked to the road in the dark, blocking out what she was leaving behind, and feeling a faint pleasure in being by herself. The stars were still out, and it suited her that they were so bright and serene, and yet so distant. It was not long before she saw the bounce of headlights as the milk truck made its way slowly along the icy road. She stood sideways to the lights as the vehicle approached, and when it stopped went immediately to the back. The hired man was standing in the big doorway, and helped her up. There was a wooden box near the door and he pointed and said, "You can sit over there for now, but I'll have to move ya when we get loaded up."

His voice was cold and impersonal, and his abrupt manner made her feel her presence was an intrusion. She sat down without speaking, and there were no more words during the trip. He had treated her like a piece of unwanted cargo, and there was nothing she could do now except stay out of his way.

By the time they neared town it was daylight. As she stood at the back, gazing out the door at the passing December landscape, it occurred to her that the colour had pretty much gone out of everything. Along the ditch the stripped stalks and stems of old growth protruded starkly through the snow. The last blush of summer green had long since been covered over, and apart from the dull orange of swamp juniper, and the faint yellow of lichen on the grey trunks of old poplars, the countryside seemed altogether drab and subdued. The harbour was still open, but even that would soon snap shut.

As they drove at last through the streets of Charlottetown she observed all the houses with pretty decorations in the windows and wreaths on the doors. She hadn't been to Charlotte-town since her trip in on the train several years earlier; and now, as then, she felt out of place. It seemed a long way from Bear River, and the small sagging house which had become the centre of her confined world.

When the truck pulled into the dairy she clambered down and asked the driver when he would be heading back. He said he had to pick up some "truck" at the wholesalers, and at Ca-nada Packers, and that after that he would be having his dinner at the hotel. He didn't men-tion the bootlegger, but she knew from the talk around home that he would almost certainly be stopping there sometime before he left the city. He was usually quite drunk by the time he returned in the evening, and in Bear River everyone wondered how he managed to keep the truck on the road. But as far as anyone knew he had never had an accident, or paid a fine.

"I'm not exactly sure when we'll be pulling out," he concluded, "but you probably should be back here by two o'clock, or a little before."

It took her a few minutes to walk uptown. Not knowing where to go from there she stood for a short time outside Holman's on Grafton Street, almost paralysed by her fear, and the daunting prospect of having to ask a complete stranger for directions to the Unemployment Office. Realizing she didn't have much time she finally stopped a woman in a long brown cloth coat; one who seemed as poor as herself. "Oh yes, dear," the woman replied kindly, "you're almost there. It's just up the street to the corner and another block down."

When she stepped inside the office there were several people in front of the wicket, lined up like grey birds of winter on a bare limb, waiting their turn at the feeder. She took her place in the queue without looking at anyone's face, and as the line moved forward she began to feel a very great tightness in her chest. It was all she could do to keep from fleeing, but she remembered the long trip in the truck, and the children waiting at home, and began to go over in her mind what she would say.

The middle-aged woman behind the counter had a large Christmas corsage on her smooth white blouse, made up of shiny green leaves and waxed red berries. She wore a pair of glasses with tiny rhinestones in the upper corners, and her perfectly grey hair was styled neatly in some kind of bob; so neatly, that the overall effect was one of prim severity. As she moved nearer, the woman from Bear River found herself wishing it was a man she was approaching.

Finally, it was her turn. She told the woman her name, and where she was from. "I'm expect-ing a cheque any day," she explained, "but I need the money for Christmas. I heard that the cheques come in here before they're mailed out to the country, so I came in this morning . . . . "

The woman broke in, interrupting her before she could finish her rehearsed explanation. "We can't do that," she said curtly, "the cheques aren't due for almost a week. It's impossible to get them now. You'll just have to wait, I'm sorry."

The words stunned her.

She wanted to say more, or at least have a chance to explain, but the woman's blunt response had left no opening. She remained there, dumbfounded, for just a moment, and then turned and walked to the door, her eyes downcast and her head bowed. There was little anger in her, or feeling of any kind. The encounter had left her numb, and like a dog turned outdoors she went outside and just stood there.

There had been many times during the previous few years when she had felt at the end of her resources; many days when she felt so little power in herself she could scarcely breathe. On those days, when it seemed she might disappear entirely beneath the surface of her own salted grief, it was the children who saved her, or at least kept her going. And now, standing motionless on the sidewalk in Charlottetown, it was the same. The thought of her children, waiting for Santa Claus, made it impossible not to act. There was nothing left for her now but to take what she needed, and as she set off up the street towards Woolworth's she determined what she would do.

The store was crowded with shoppers, and filled with the aroma of freshly made doughnuts, arranged on trays at the bakery counter between the two front doors. Her heart pounded as she walked among the aisles, and stopped in front of the stationery and school supplies. There were pencils there, and packages of crayons, and as she slipped two of each into the pocket of her coat she resolved to send the payment by mail the day her cheque arrived. There were now four gifts in her possession, but she needed three more. She thought she should probably leave, and go to another store, but when she turned her head to see if anyone was looking, and noted that the other people in the store seemed preoccupied with their own shopping, she decided to finish what she had started.

Thinking of combs or barrettes for the girls, she moved around the end of the aisle and made her way to the cosmetics department. She believed her presence in the store had gone unnoted, but could not have known that her shabby appearance, along with the clear language of her carriage and movements, had made her stand out conspicuously in the experienced eyes of the manager. As she was slipping the three small hair clasps into the same pocket, he moved quickly to her side and took her by the elbow. "What are you doing?" he asked accusingly.

She was speechless, and the breath went out of her, as though she had just been struck a tremendous blow in the stomach. The man waited just a moment, expecting some kind of response, but when it became obvious the woman wasn't going to say anything, he ordered her to come with him to the store office. She followed him, dazed with fright, and when he asked her to empty the contents of her pocket onto the desk, she obeyed mechanically.

"Do you have the money to pay for these?" he asked.

She didn't speak — just gave her head a quick, barely perceptible shake.

"Then I'm going to have to call the police," he said, reaching for the phone. "Lady, you can't just pick up things and walk out of here, you know," he added, as though to convince himself of the necessity of the call.

The woman collapsed into a chair, like a person before a judge who has just received the death sentence.

It had been a routine morning at the police station. Two of the men on duty had returned with one of the well-known downtown "derelicts" who had slipped on a patch of ice outside Moore and MacLeod's and opened a deep gash on his forehead. They had taken him to the doctor for stitches and he was now in the station lock-up where he would spend Christmas Eve. There would be others with him before the day was over; men who had no better prospects for the holiday than a small cot and a free meal within the warm, familiar confines of the police station.

The year before, these same two policemen had gone out on Christmas Eve and brought back some chicken sandwiches and a few bottles of pop from the Island Grill. They had organized a party of sorts for the five men in the lock-up, and had even brought in a guitar and sang a few carols. It was a sorry, comical affair, but the incarcerated men were touched by the gesture, and, after Christmas, when they were back on the street, had told everyone in town about their experience. Further, it seemed likely that on this Christmas, a year later, some of those men would be back in the same place, hoping for a repeat performance. It would become, they hoped, a Christmas tradition.

Hanging up the phone the officer at the desk turned to the two policemen and said, "That was Woolworth's. The manager's got a shoplifter in his office and wants someone to go down and take care of it. He caught some poor wretch with her pockets full, and no money to pay for anything."

"Somebody doing her Christmas shopping the cheap way," laughed one of the cops.

"Why doesn't he just forget about it?" replied the other, without moving out of his chair, "It's Christmas Eve, for God's sake!"

"I suggested that," said the man at the desk, "but he says there's just too much stuff walkin' out the door, and that he has to put a stop to it. I think he wants to press charges."

The two veteran policemen had seen it all over the years, and had become accustomed to the various patterns of despair of men and women who had become the victims of their own desperation. The job required a thick skin. You could break up a fight, arrest a thief, or intervene in a domestic quarrel, but you soon discovered that in most cases there was little you could do to change the patterns. It was like mopping the same soiled floor day after day, and you learned it was easier to go to work if you kept your hands out of the dirty water. But there were exceptions, and on that Christmas Eve day, when the two policemen walked into the office of the manager and saw the accused woman, they sensed immediately that this was one of them.

She was obviously terrified, and had drawn herself together into as small a space as possible. Bent slightly forward in the chair, her legs were together, with one foot on top of the other, and her red, chapped hands clasped together on her lap, on top of an old black purse. She looked up furtively when they came through the door, but immediately dropped her eyes and began to rock back and forth.

"What's the problem here?" asked the first policeman through the door.

"I caught this woman stealing from the store," replied the manager, from his seat behind the desk. "She's the third one this week, and I've got to clamp down on it."

The words "clamp down" were especially frightening to the woman. She knew she was guilty, and that she had no money to pay a fine. The only thing she could think was that they would probably put her in jail. She knew what it was to feel abandoned, and the thought of her own children, alone and unattended on Christmas Eve, not knowing where their mother had gone, was excruciating. There was a howl of protest in her which longed for expression, but she kept her teeth together, and her mouth shut. Now, as ever, it seemed impossible to fight back, or to give vent to her compacted pain.

"What did she take?" asked the policeman.

The manager pointed to the small collection of items on the desk. "That's how much she had when I caught her, but who knows how much she would have taken if I hadn't seen what was going on."

The officer turned and looked at his partner, and then back at the manager. "What's it worth?" he asked.

"Ninety-seven cents."

"Jesus, Mary and Joseph!" interjected the second policeman, "you want to press charges for ninety-seven cents?"

"Well what am I supposed to do, just let people walk in here and take whatever they want and then walk out? This is a store you know, not a charity depot."

The first policeman turned again and looked at the other.

"I wasn't going to take anything else," the woman said softly in a pleading tone. "I have seven children waiting at home, and no presents, and all I wanted was one little thing for each of them. And I know you might not believe it, but I was going to send the money in the mail next week. I'm expectin' a cheque but it didn't get here in time for Christmas."

The manager shifted uncomfortably in his seat, with a look on his face which said, "I've heard all this before." He was about to say something when the first policeman spoke.

"If we give you the ninety-seven cents will you forget about the charges?"

There was a long pause.

"All right, all right," replied the manager, "but tell her she is never to set foot in this store again, and if she does I will be watching her like a hawk."

Ignoring the man's comments the policeman took out his wallet and tossed a dollar bill onto the desk. "Keep the change," he added sarcastically.

He then gathered up the crayons and the other items and handed them to the woman. "Put these in your purse,"he said, "and please come with us. You can tell us about it back at the station."

The woman stiffened, and when he saw that his words had caused new fright he softened his voice and attempted to reassure her. "We're not going to lay charges, Madam, but we need to talk with you for just a few minutes. Don't worry, everything's going to be all right."

There was kindness and understanding in the man's voice, and it reminded her of the woman on the street who had given her directions, but as she walked down the block to the police station in the company of the two policemen she felt embarrassed and tongue-tied. When one of them asked her where she lived she said, "Bear River, near Souris," but couldn't think of another thing to say. Fortunately it was a short walk, and she was relieved when they arrived at the station and the men escorted her directly to a small room with no one in it, and pulled the door almost shut behind them.

She was invited to have a seat, and one of the cops asked her if she would like a cup of coffee. "Yes," she replied, "if it's not too much trouble."

"No trouble at all," he said, and left the room.

It was almost noon, and she hadn't eaten anything all day, so when the policeman returned with coffee, and a doughnut, she responded gratefully. "Oh, thank you! Thank you very much!" she said, feeling slightly less apprehensive, even though she was still unsure why they had brought her back to the station, or what was going to happen next. She remembered the seven small gifts in her purse, and her worst fear was that she might have to give them up.

"It's true what I said about the cheque," she volunteered, "and if I can keep these presents for the children I'll send you the money next week."

"Don't give it another thought," replied the man who had paid the dollar. "The reason we asked you to come here is to find out more about your children. Maybe we can help out with your Christmas. How old are they?"

As she listed off their names and ages he copied it all down on a notepad. "Do you have a husband?" he asked.

"Yes," she replied, "but he hasn't had any work all fall."

She was relieved when he moved on to another question. The reference to her husband had created a new consternation in her, and she could feel her arms and legs beginning to tremble unaccountably. Her feelings about her husband were largely buried, but the cop's question had opened the door to that sealed chamber, and it was with some difficulty that she managed to shut it again.

"How did you get into town?" he asked.

"I came in on the back of the milk truck."

"And is that how you're going back?"

"Yes," she replied, "and I have to be at the dairy by quarter to two or I'll miss my ride."

"Well that doesn't leave us much time," he responded, pushing up his coat sleeve and looking at his watch. "You just sit tight. We'll make some calls and see if we can round up some toys for those kids of yours."

Within a few minutes the two officers had contacted the President of the Kinsmen Club, the Captain at the Salvation Army, and the Sister in charge at Catholic Social Services. While the woman sat alone in the room, still in a state of shock from her experience at Woolworth's, they made the rounds. Arriving at the station just before one, they came back into the room, their arms loaded with food. They were both conspicuously pleased with themselves. Their uniforms were the wrong colour, but with their red cheeks, and their faces fairly shining with goodwill, they looked for all the world like two Santa Clauses in blue. Further, they were no sooner in the door when a man from the Kinsmen Club arrived on the scene with two large cardboard cartons filled with toys.

"This is all for you," they announced proudly. "There are a couple of toys for each of the children, and two turkey dinners complete with all the trimmings."

"And we've got something else for you," one of them added, reaching into his pocket.

The woman didn't realize it, but the story of her misadventure, and of her seven children waiting at home in Bear River for the arrival of Santa Claus, had spread quickly throughout the police station. Even the Chief heard all about it and was, like the rest, moved by the story. When the two good Samaritans told him they were taking up a collection for the woman he immediately reached into his pocket. His donation, along with the contributions of virtually everyone else at the station, amounted to thirty-seven dollars, and it was this sum that the policeman handed to the overwhelmed woman. The unanticipated generosity of these strangers was almost more than she could comprehend. She couldn't say anything, but the look of surprise and amazement on her face did not go unnoticed by her two benefactors.

Neither of the policemen had mentioned it, but their call to the Catholic Social Services had confirmed the truth of her story about her children and the wretched circumstances of their homelife; further, they had learned that two of the children were diabetic, and that the husband was an alcoholic who contributed little or nothing to the care of his large family. And so it surprised her somewhat when the policeman made a point of saying, "This money is for you. No one else needs to know a thing about it. No one!"

The insinuation was clear.

It was shortly after two when the milk truck pulled up outside the dairy. When the woman pointed it out to the policeman, he got out of the car. During the time they had sat waiting he had told her a little about himself. He enjoyed talking about his own little girls, and how excited they were about Christmas. Earlier in the day, when they were leaving Woolworth's, he had introduced himself and his partner, but in the panic of the moment she hadn't picked up on the names. She now wanted very much to know who they were, but couldn't bring herself to ask.

"You stay here for just a minute," he said as he closed the door, "I want to have a few words with the driver."

She watched as he walked slowly to the truck, and could see the taut look on the face of the driver as the policeman approached him. He got out of the truck and the two men had a brief conversation. They then walked back over to the car and began removing the boxes from the back seat. She made a move to get out, but the cop told her to stay inside where it was warm.

When everything was loaded into the back of the truck he came back and opened her door. "I had a word with him," he reported, nodding his head in the direction of the driver, "and he said you can ride up front on the way home. The fella who came in the cab has agreed to ride in the box."

He spoke matter-of-factly, but she would discover months later that he had insisted on the new riding arrangement, and that when the driver hesitated he had been warned menacingly that if he didn't comply he could look forward to being pulled over and checked every time he came to town.

He walked her to the truck, and before she climbed up into the cab she thanked him again for his kindness. He touched her lightly on the shoulder and smiled. "I'm just glad we could help," he said, "and I hope you and your kids have a Merry Christmas." She never saw him again.

The trip home alongside the sullen driver was almost as mute as the trip in, but she was grateful for the silence, and wrapped it around herself like a protective shawl. Mile after mile she reflected on the day, and determined to write a letter to the police station expressing her gratitude. Each time she recalled the gifts and the food in the back of the truck, and the money in her purse, it sent a wave of delight through her entire body. She returned to the thought again and again, fondling it happily the way a child caresses a new toy.

When she was away from home she often dreaded her return. But tonight it was different. As the truck neared Bear River she began to think about the supper she would prepare, and how she would hide the gifts. There was a small building near the road about a hundred yards before her own gate. It was an old forge where, in earlier years, the horses in the community had been shod, and broken wheels restored to roundness. No one used it anymore, and she decided it would be a good place to get out.

She pointed out the place to the driver and he pulled over and stopped. She thanked him for the chance to Town. "It looks like a big Christmas at your place," said one of the men in the back as he handed down the boxes. There was some envy in his voice, and she wondered about his circumstances, and what he had waiting at home.

He asked her if he could help with the carrying, but she declined. She wanted to be alone with the packages, and was looking forward to the prospect of carrying each of them into the old forge, and exploring there the full extent of her good fortune.

When everything was inside she went through the contents of the boxes. There would be no presents for her on Christmas day, and no pretty ornaments in her windows, but there, kneeling in that dilapidated building, in the stillness and soft last-light of Christmas Eve, surrounded by the bounty of others' kindness, and filled with the certain anticipation of her children's delight, she experienced the full grandeur of Christmas joy.

When the happy task of sorting was finished, she took the money from her purse and hid it beneath a board in the corner, near the place where the old canvas bellows once fanned the nutcoal embers into bright heat. She left behind the toys and the two turkeys. Later, when the children were asleep, she would return for them, but for now she filled the largest carton with the potatoes and vegetables, the oranges and apples, the package of tea, the cans of milk, the pudding, and the bag of hard candy. It was a heavy load, but pleasant to carry.

As she walked down the road toward her laneway she could see the light of a lamp in her window, and the outline of a child looking out. The stars were appearing overhead, and in the frosty silence of the darkening countryside she took pleasure in the white bursting forth of her breath, and the crunch of her feet on the frozen road.

GIFTS

"We'd get, you know, what we got — we were quite satisfied with it."

Grand Tracadie

"Mom went on the train to Charlottetown for her Christmas shopping. She took $3.00. That money was used for Christmas treats, gifts for the seven children - and the train fare. And, you know, there was a special package under the tree for everyone of us that year."

St. Columba

"I'd go downstairs with Daddy. He'd be going to do the milking and he'd light the fire. I can remember getting this bottle of pink nail polish — how excited I was about that, showing it to him. I can also remember getting the big box of crayons — I think there were sixty-four in it. Oh, the colours were too pretty — the turquoise, and the purples and all that! What a big deal that was."

DeSable

"They used to go with the stuff [presents] to the granary, and bury it down into the oats, and then at the last of it, when they would bring things in, little grains of oats would fall on the floor. I would say, well how was that, but they would make up excuses."

Cardigan

"One year I got this little goose. It had wooden wheels under it on either side and an eccentric axel, you know, an axel with a twist in it. The twisted part was attached to the goose's neck, and every time the axel turned the goose's neck went in and out. It was great."

Miminegash

The Christmas Orange

erhaps the greatest difference between Christmas today and Christmas years ago is that back then people were poor. Not that there aren't any poor today, but then everyone was poor — or almost everyone. It wasn't a grinding, end-of-the-rope kind of poverty. Most everyone had food enough to eat and warm clothes to wear. The woodshed was filled with wood, the cellar with potatoes and carrots, and the pickle barrel with herring or pork. There were strings of dried apples hanging from the attic rafters, and a carcass of frozen beef hanging in the shed. In many ways it was an era of plenty, so you might say that rural Islanders weren't poor, they just didn't have much money.

What strikes me forcibly when I speak to some older people is that the scarcity of money made it possible to receive very great pleasure from simple, inexpensive things. I know, for example, that for many children an orange, a simple orange, was a Christmas miracle. It was the perfect golden ball of legend and fairy tale which appeared, as if by magic, on December 25th. In that drab homespun world of grey and brown, it shone mightily like a small sun. According to one ancient legend, an anonymous benefactor dropped gold coins down the chimney of a poor family and they accidently fell into a stocking which was hanging near the hearth. The Christmas orange of later centuries was said to represent the gold in the toe of that stocking.

The orange was a kind of incarnation of Christmas itself, and for many Islanders the most vivid, evocative memory of the blessed season is the memory of an orange on Christmas morning. One woman from a large family in Morell said that at her home you were fortunate if you received a whole orange for yourself. She recalled some lean years when she received half an orange, and was happy for it.

For children who ate oatmeal porridge for breakfast virtually every day of their lives, and had molasses on bread most days in their school lunch; for children who looked at fried pota-toes almost every evening for supper and considered turnip scrapings a special evening snack;

for these children an orange was a marvel, something almost too wonderful and prized to be eaten — an exotic, sensuous wonder.

One woman confessed that she kept her orange for a week after Christmas: kept it in a drawer. Several times a day she would go to her hiding place and take out the orange just to fondle it, and smell it, and to anticipate joyously the pleasure which was to come. Eventually it had to be eaten: deliberately, unhurriedly, ceremoniously and gratefully. Piece by piece, and finally the peeling — it was all eaten, and it was all good. All that remained was the hope that there would be another Christmas and, if God would would be so kind, another orange.

A knock on the door is a most suspenseful thing.

Inside the walls of home is a space well known: a small place under strict management. The world outside is a different story. It is vast, unpredictable and full of surprises, and there is only a door between.

Knock! Knock!

The outside wants in.

Knock! Knock! Knock!

Has the caller arrived with a message that could change the day, or even your life? Or is it a mere distraction — a nuisance and a bother?

Knock! Knock!

Who's there? What do they want? Is it an Angel or the Devil who has come, and is it for giving or taking that the visitor stands outside the door?

There are few sounds in life that can so kindle interest, and light up anticipation, as a rap on the door, and it's not surprising to me that door-knocking was ritualized in the folkways of some of our ancestors. They had an uncanny knack for dramatization: a sure instinct for transforming the homely, everyday events of life into scenes of ceremonial significance. The Scots, in particular, seemed to have been especially good at this sort of household pageantry, and when they came to Prince Edward Island they brought with them a number of ancient holiday "knocking" customs which had been practised for centuries. Most of them have disappeared from the landscape of our present-day celebrations, but a few have survived in the memories of older Islanders.

A woman who grew up near Crapaud recalled that on Christmas morning her household was always awakened early, sometimes around six o'clock, by a visitor known as "the Lucky Bird." This early-morning caller, usually a boy from the community, would rap on the door and greet whoever answered with a rhyme.

Merry Christmas,
and a Happy New Year.
A pocketful of money,
and a cellar full of beer.

The child was rewarded with a dime, which was given in the hope that good luck would befall the household during the ensuing year. Apparently other children would arrive later and recite the same rhyme, but it was only the first visitor, "the Lucky Bird," who received the coin. The late-comers were, however, rewarded with a treat, and a "better luck next year."

It was not Christmas, but New Year's, which seems to have been the occasion when most of these old customs and superstitions were practised. Louis MacDonald of Cornwall told me that on New Year's Eve his mother would bake a special sweet bannock, filled with raisins and currants, and that when it came out of the oven, while still hot, she would wrap it in a cloth and take it to the door and thump it against the door frame, all the while reciting an old Gaelic rhyme which translates, "May no harm come to this house from this night, until this night twelve months."

According to Louis the family members would then put homemade butter on the warm bannock, pour glasses of milk, and enjoy their special New Year's treat, secure in the knowledge that only good would come through the door, and that " . . . the home and family had been properly blessed for the coming year."

In many Scottish communities there was also a tradition which attached great significance to the gender of the first visitor on New Year's Day. I have heard many variations on this tradition, but the common thread was the belief that it was good luck to the household if the first visitor was a dark-haired man, and bad luck if it was a woman. One woman recalled that on New Year's Day her grandmother would lock all the doors to the house to prevent the inadvertent entrance of a female.

Gertie Nicholson, from Valleyfield, was told by her grandmother that it was an especially bad omen for the coming year if the first visitor to a home on New Year's Day was by a dark-haired female. She informed me, somewhat ruefully, that she was, "the black one in the family," and that, consequently, she felt obliged to stay home the entire day while everyone else went visiting. Such was the power of the belief.

Eileen Duffy, who grew up in Tracadie, related that when she was a little girl there was a man from the community, Joe MacIsaac, who came to her house on New Year's Eve and banged on the outside walls. Apparently he went around the structure rapping and thumping the shingles with a stick. His unsolicited performance created a considerable racket, but apparently the ritual purpose of the noisy deed was to drive away all evil spirits from the house, and from the family inside, for the coming year. When he was finished he was, of course, welcomed inside for a visit and a holiday treat.

This memory from Tracadie sounds remarkably similar to a custom in the North Shore community of Monticello. In Monticello, New Year's Eve was also known as "Coolick's Night." Father Wendell MacIntyre who grew up there said that in his boyhood the children in the community would go to various homes on New Year's Eve and make a noise by "pulling a stick or an old picket down the shingles." When the residents would come to the door they would be invited in for a treat — "a cookie or some other goodie, whatever they had."

Jimmie "Bornish" MacDonald, who still lives in Monticello, also remembers the Cooligers. He told me that about six o'clock on New Year's Eve in the early 1900s the children of the community would band together and go from one house to the next, "scratching on the doors of the houses with a stick." He doesn't recall that anyone ever put on a disguise for these house-to-house forays, but Teresa Wilson, from neighbouring Goose River, was told by her grandfather that in his day people would dress up in masks and old clothing in order to disguise themselves from their neighbours. She was also told that while the Cooligers were chanting their song they would be "rubbing straw brooms and horse tails against the house," and that if they were ever refused entry, "they would threaten to cast a spell on the house."

Teresa recalls, as well, the verse chanted by the Cooligers.

Come out old woman,
and shake your feathers,
we hope you don't think
that we're all beggars.
We're boys and girls
who've come out to play,
give us a treat,
and we'll go away.

A variation on the rhyme was obtained by Teresa from a neighbour.

Get up old woman,
and shake your feathers,
you needn't think
that we are beggars.

> We're little children,
> and we came to play,
> so on with your kettle,
> and down with your pan,
> haul out your black bottle,
> and give us a dram.

The reference to the "black bottle" would seem to point to an earlier time when the visitors on Coolick's Night were adults, looking for strong drink; however, in the final years of the practice in Monticello it seems to have become, for the most part, a pastime for the youngsters of the community.

If the rhyme was performed to the satisfaction of the hosts, which it invariably was, the visitors were invited in for a treat, perhaps a piece of cake or "one of those delicious black molasses cookies." When it had been consumed, they were off to another house for another performance. "We didn't stay long," recalled Jimmie, "just long enough to fill our bellies. We really looked forward to it," he concluded, "the way the young people look forward to Christmas today."

It has been two centuries now since the first Scots arrived on these shores, with their considerable baggage of inherited custom. Much of that legacy has been lost, and though we are still roused frequently during the holidays by beckoning knocks on the door, the rag-tag crew of Cooligers appears no more on steps and porches. The knock of ancient tradition has largely ceased, and the sing-song chant of those New Year's revellers is a faint, disappearing sound, as distant and obscured as Highland peaks, wrapped in the misted veil of faded recollection.

Note: My spelling of "Cooligers" is a phonetic rendition of the way the word is currently pronounced by those who still use it. In the Gaelic it was spelled "Cuileagars," and has the root meaning "to fly around."

GIFTS

"Some children wouldn't tell their parents what they wanted, because they knew they had no money for toys. So the children kept their wishes to themselves."

Alberry Plains

"She remembers her grandpa making her a toy she referred to as 'jumping jacks' out of the breastbone of a goose. He had a way that he could put the bones together, working with them some way, and putting string around them — and he put a stick on it too. Somehow we used to wind it up, then we would put it on the floor and it would jump around."

Bangor

"Father used to make tops out of old thread spools, and then dye them different colours, with the dyes mother used to dye the sweaters she knitted. All the children got these every year, and every top was a different colour."

East Baltic

"Every Christmas morning was always the same. My parents gave us kids these small cups, smaller than tea cups. On Christmas Eve we would put them out, and when we got up on Christmas morning they would be full of candies. That would be our Christmas present, and we would all be so excited about our candies."

Summerside

"Garfield got Ralph [his son] a fiddle one Christmas, and instead of just putting it under the tree or by the stocking he got up very early, lit the stove, and then began playing. That brought Ralph running downstairs in a hurry."

High Bank

The Animals

Jesus our brother, kind and good,
was humbly born in stable rude;
The friendly beasts around him stood,
Jesus our brother, kind and good.
And every beast, by some good spell,
In the dark stable was glad to tell,
Of the gift he gave Immanuel,
The gift he gave Immanuel.

From "The Friendly Beasts," Author unknown

It is always difficult with legends that have been transmitted orally for hundreds of years to discern their original meaning. I suspect, however, that the Christmas legend of the devout animals, which survived on Prince Edward Island into the twentieth century, was a legend born out of a sense that the story of the nativity is one which has significance, not only for humans, but for the entire creation. At least that's what I like to think.

I have encountered this Christmas legend many times over the years. Mickey Place told me about it, and Walter Shaw mentioned it in his book *Tell Me The Tales*. Although both remembrances obviously derive from the same legend, there is a variation in the accounts. Mickey, who heard the story from his grandmother, said that at midnight on Christmas Eve all the cows in the cow stable got down on their knees. He also added, ominously, that if anyone tried to witness the event the cows would remain standing, and that the person who thwarted their devotion would be dead before the next Christmas. In Shaw's account the cattle all went to their knees on Christmas morning and lowed softly.

A woman who was raised in Mt. Mellick was told by her father that if you went to the barn at midnight on Christmas Eve you would see one single cow standing guard, waiting for Jesus, while the other animals slept. And in the Palmer's Road district it was believed that on Christmas Eve the animals were given the gift of speech, and talked to one another, presumably about that first Christmas, long ago, when members of their species had been privileged onlookers to the holy birth. The farmers in that area made certain all their chores were completed before dark so they would not have to intrude upon this unusual phenomenon. I also heard of one father who advised his children solemnly that all the animals in the barn kneeled at twelve o'clock on Christmas Eve, but that if anyone dared to look they would be struck blind and dumb.

The threats of certain death, or of being struck blind and dumb, stand out starkly in the otherwise gentle narrative, like harshly discordant notes in a lullaby, or the heavy dark lines children sometimes draw across pictures of smiling adults. I was intrigued by this dark side of the legend, and took my puzzlement to a wise friend, whose judgements I respect on such matters.

We eventually concluded that the references may reveal an intuitive insight into what a great shock it would be to our whole world-view if animals were seen to be devout. The sharp line of distinction we have drawn between ourselves and the "dumb beasts," a line so fundamental to our perception of nature, would disappear in that moment, and it would be impossible for us ever to see, or to speak, in the same way again. "It's our view of ourselves that would die," he concluded, "and we'd be forced to go back to an older way of looking at the world, and our place in it."

In the religious lore of many peoples the animals occupy a prominent place. Certainly in the cosmology of the Micmac people, who occupied Prince Edward Island when the Europeans arrived, animals such as the bear, the beaver and the whale are included in almost every story. These legends recall that stage in human consciousness when the indisputable interdependence between animals and humans was still a matter of mythic significance; a time before humans began to imagine themselves an elevated, lordly class with both the power and the right to treat animals in any manner that pleased them.

According to Christmas legend, Jesus was born in a stable, and while there is no actual mention in the Gospels of the animals that might have been there, over the years they have become an essential part of the Christmas scene. The floppy ears of the ass, the doleful eyes of the cow, and the woolly profile of the sheep are standard props in every manger scene in every churchyard and shopping mall throughout the Western World. They're an integral part of the scene, but, as far as I can tell, not really an integral part of the story.

I recall the time, about ten years ago, I was asked to tell a story to the children at church during the annual Christmas Eve service. I decided to talk about the animals. By taking certain liberties with the New Testament accounts, I contrived to fill the stable with a wide variety of both furry and feathered creatures, each of which was given a voice whereby it was able to express its own particular response to the coming of the Holy child. My overall intention, if I remember correctly, was to suggest that the story of the incarnation — of God become flesh — had an application which might very well extend beyond the boundary of our own species. Humans, after all, aren't the only ones with flesh.

One observation I wanted to make, but didn't, was that the appearance of the Divine in the form of a lamb, a chickadee, or even a mouse, would also have been a powerful sign of the inherent sacredness of all life. I judged that the adults probably weren't quite ready for that; and, if the truth were known, I probably wasn't quite ready for it myself. The children, of course, wouldn't have had the slightest problem.

Following the service a prominent member of the church, concern evident in his face, took me to one side. His manner was courteous, but there was an unmistakable reprimand in his comments. He wondered why, on Christmas Eve, I had chosen to deflect attention from the Christ-child by talking about the imaginary animals. I tried to explain that, in my opinion, my remarks were entirely in keeping with the Christmas message, and that the sheep, no less than the shepherds, might be considered celebrants of the event. But it was obvious that, in his opinion, I had strayed too far from the essential storyline. But had I? More and more it seems clear to me that a Christmas storyline which cannot incorporate the animals, and all the other creatures as well, is a storyline which leaves out too much.

Years ago, no less than today, the animals were the principal donors and supporters of the Christmas celebrations. There was Christmas dinner, courtesy of the goose and the duck; meat pie, courtesy of the rabbit; Christmas doughnuts, blood sausages and pothead, courtesy of the pig; pudding, cake and cookies, courtesy of the hen; homemade ice cream, courtesy of the cow; and a ride to Midnight Mass, wrapped in layers of warm winter wool, courtesy of the horse and the sheep. The contribution of these creatures was great, and many of them, in imitation of the Saviour himself, gave their lives. And what did these donors receive in return? In most cases, not so much as a nod of the head or a passing reference in the prayers and liturgy. The extent of the ingratitude was astounding.

There were a few exceptions. Frank Ledwell in his book, *The North Shore of Home*, tells of an exemplary priest in St. Peter's who gave a memorable annual homily on the topic of Christmas joy, in which he included reverent mention of the fish in the sea and the animals in the farmyard. On some farms extra feed and deeper bedding were provided for the animals on Christmas Eve, and I was told of one farmer who braided his horse's tail and mane with red ribbon for the yearly trip to the Christmas Concert. But that was about it. For the most part the animals, their donations notwithstanding, were pretty much taken for granted. But my mind goes back to those kneeling cows in the barn, and the intuition of at least some of our forebears, that the concentric circles of adoration, radiating out from the Christmas Crib, are meant to encompass every creature.

The Christmas Concert

Every year we like to say it,
Every year we mean it too,
Merry Christmas friends and neighbours,
Merry Christmas to you.

Christmas recitation by Grade One pupils
Blooming Point schoolhouse, c. 1948

t was the closest thing to a gala occasion that many rural folk would ever attend; the most important, eagerly anticipated event on the social calendar. The entire community turned out in its Sunday best. Everyone who could move, or be moved, would be packed into the little one-room school house, or community hall, which for that night was transformed into a centre for the performing arts. It was, of course, the Christmas Concert.

In many communities the momentous event was referred to as "the Christmas Tree," which harks back to a period, early in the century, before it became the custom to display trees in the homes. The only decorated tree many children would see was the one at the concert, and, while the phrase, "going to the Christmas Tree," may sound strange to modern ears, at that time the words were an altogether accurate description of the experience.

One woman from Monticello said that "going to the Christmas Tree was like a child going to New York today." She recalled that when she first attended the annual concert at age five she had never seen a Christmas tree before, and that it was "like stepping into fantasy land."

"I was never so overjoyed in my life," she added, "and to this day, when I see a Christmas tree, it still gives me that same, incredible feeling."

The teacher, poor thing, was artistic director, production supervisor and stage manager all rolled into one. For her it was, quite literally, a trial. Any teacher who couldn't put together a good Christmas concert just wouldn't last long. As one former teacher told me, "You had to have a good concert, or woe betide you!" She also had to have a present for each of the students, and one man recalled that in his community the teacher worked for two weeks during potato digging time for $1.50 a day in order to have extra money for the pupils' gifts.

Weeks of preparation were required, during which time ordinary lessons were all but suspended. One teacher from Dover admitted this was the case in her school, but said that getting ready for the concert was an education in itself. "Some might say we were neglecting our school subjects," she mused, "but I always felt it gave us the extracurricular studies of drama, elocution and music; yes, and sewing, too, because the girls would help to make the costumes, sometimes out of crêpe paper in all different colours."

Then, finally, when all the lines were memorized, all the costumes made, all the spruce garlands and tissue-paper roses in place, and a stage improvised at the front of the room, the big night arrived.

How delightfully the rustic splendour of the scene stands out in memory. I recall the nickering of horses and ringing of sleigh bells in the schoolyard as people arrived, and how wonderfully bright the windows were from the gas lanterns brought from home and hung along the walls. I recall the streamers hung diagonally across the room with a red Christmas bell in the centre, and how, when it was cold, the streamers would droop down almost to the tops of the desks, but would rise up again when the school warmed. I recall the white sheets strung across the front on a piece of number nine wire, with a big, self-conscious boy at either end; and the school trustee, in his rumpled brown suit, who stood up at the start and awkwardly welcomed everyone. I recall the ten-cent packages of light and dark homemade fudge in little brown bags at intermission, and the pencil box with the sliding top which I received from the teacher. But most of all I recall the excitement of waiting for the THUMP, THUMP, THUMP, on the door. "He's here, he's here!" we would all cry out, and, with that, Santa Claus would make his grand entrance.

He didn't look at all like today's Santa Claus with his stylish costume of red and white. Santa then was quite a different, more earthy creature. He wore a heavy, knee-length fur coat, and a stocking cap, with a string of sleigh-bells around his ample waist, and a pair of new boots, just like the pair Freddie's uncle had worn to church the previous Sunday. And

58

one year, in the middle of everything, he passed out from the heat in the school and, I suspect, from the Christmas "shine" he had been sampling before his arrival. One woman from Park Corner who attended the concerts as a child reported that after all these years she can never smell rum without thinking of Santa Claus.

After the Christmas Concert the children talked about Santa for days. One man said he remembered his little friend telling him earnestly that Santa "never blinked his eyes once all evening. That's just how close he was watchin' him," he concluded.

Looking back as an adult it occurs to me that there were probably many in attendance for whom the evening was an ordeal of noise and confusion. But for a seven-year-old, who didn't even know the word, it was a night of enchantment.

There was one Christmas Concert I will never forget. That year Santa arrived carrying two bags over his shoulder, one filled with presents, and one that wriggled and jounced with some form of concealed life. "I've got a present here," he announced, "but you'll have to catch it." With that he dumped out onto the floor a small brown puppy with white paws, which began to run through the crowd. Many hands reached out for him, mine included. He came near where I was standing and, for a moment, it seemed possible I might be lucky enough to grab him. But just then a farmer standing beside me — Marshall Rayner, I believe — reached down and scooped him up. My disappointment was great, my hopes dashed. Then I heard the man say, "David, do you have a dog?" "N-No," I stammered. "Then here's something for you," he said, as he placed the frightened little creature in my arms.

It was a sublime moment, a Christmas epiphany! Further, I have the suspicion that every Christmas since then has been anticipated and silently measured against that long-ago event when God appeared on earth during the Christmas Concert in the form of a puppy. Walking home that night in the snow with the little dog in my arms I had some inkling of what the Virgin Mary might have experienced. She could not have felt more blessed.

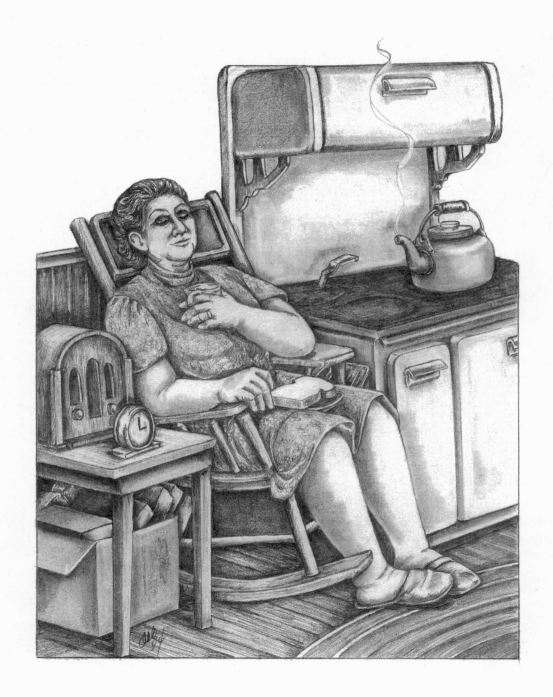

Margaret's Masterpiece

he wallpaper on her bedroom wall had one of those repetitive floral patterns where each constellation of blossoms was the same as every other, and where each connected to the next in exactly the same way. The only place it was different was in the corner, where the last piece had been cut to make it fit. The paper had been her own choice, but sometimes she would lie on her bed and squint, vainly attempting to locate one pattern which was in any way different from the rest.

Margaret had a husband, a house and five children who depended on her. There wasn't much money, but she was able to make ends meet, and, as far as she knew, there wasn't anyone who had anything bad to say about her, except for one woman up the road who had something bad to say about everyone. She knew every single person in her district by name, as well as their politics, their religion, and who their people had been; and everyone knew her in the same way. There was comfort and security in that knowing; yet, for all of that, sometimes her own life seemed blurred — unremarkable and unnoted. It wasn't anything she could explain to anyone, or even to herself, but she felt it most days. It might have been easier somehow if there had been some great disappointment in her life, or if she had been able to spend her time nursing the regret of secret dreams unfulfilled. But it wasn't like that. The regret had no name, and the discontent no particular shape.

Sometimes it occurred to her how much she was like her mother. That wasn't altogether unpleasant, but she always felt stirrings of annoyance when Ruth, her aunt, would call her by her mother's name. It was the same feeling she had when her husband would call her "Mom"; or, when shortly after her marriage, she received a letter in the mail addressed to "Mrs. John McIsaac," and stared at it for a moment, wondering who it was for.

But Margaret seldom gave way to her feelings. Like everyone around her she was, most of the time, a careful person, measuring out her emotions in pinches and teaspoonfuls, according to the recipe of inherited wisdom. She had learned early that you had to watch every penny, and every word, and that impulsive or extravagant behaviour of any kind was the surest way of inviting criticism. Once, early in her marriage, she had sent away in the catalogue for a set of ruffled white curtains for the dining room window, and was chastised by her mother-in-law. "Well, Margaret," she said with affected nonchalance, "I'm surprised you've spent your money this way. There might be a day coming when you'll wish you had it for something else, something you really need." She paused for just a moment and then added, "I'm sure they would look lovely, but the ones that are there would be considered perfectly fine by most." It stung, and after that Margaret kept the curtains hidden away in a bureau drawer.

Margaret's house, like her own life, was tidy and neat, but largely unadorned by anything which might be considered profusive or showy. The virtue of constraint was reinforced habitually, and eventually manifested itself in all her ways. But there was one notable exception to all of this. Margaret discovered that there was one day of the year when it was possible, without reprimand, to cast aside the everyday strictures of prudence, and to let loose in an outpouring of unstinting excess. That day was Christmas Eve.

The preparation began in the fall. She'd get her fruit cakes done before the end of October, wrap them in white cotton and put them in cake tins with some slices of apple to keep them moist. Then she'd put them in the cellar, in the wall, where her husband had cut out a special niche. As adults her children could still remember going down to the cellar and opening the lids, just to smell the cakes, and to anticipate the feast which, they knew, was already taking shape in their mother's mind.

As Christmas approached, her pantry shelves would begin to fill up with all the ingredients she would need: extra sugar and flour, raisins, dates, currants, cinnamon, suet and all the rest. Then, the day before Christmas Eve, she'd get her rabbits. The skinning and gutting took place in the barn, and it always amazed her children how she could perform the task with so little mess. One of them would hold the legs while she took a razor blade and made one neat stroke down the belly so that everything would fall out in one piece. One of her sons remembered that his arms would get sore, the way they would when he held the skein of yarn, but that his mother would make the time pass quickly by telling stories about when she was a girl and had to do the same thing.

About four o'clock on Christmas Eve she'd begin to panic. There was so much left to do. She'd instruct the children to get out all her good dishes, clean them, and set them on the big table which she had covered with the white Christmas tablecloth, with roses handstitched in the corners. Both leaves of the table were up, providing a large enough space for all the food which would make an appearance before midnight. While all this was happening she'd be making her pies — lemon, apple and raisin. All the old men loved raisin.

One year her oldest daughter, in an attempt to be helpful, proceeded to cut the pies short-ly after they had come out of the oven. Her mother intervened sharply. "Not now! Not now!" she scolded. The girl did not understand that her mother's Christmas Eve event was more than a meal. It was a pageant, and cutting the pies before the company arrived did not fit the script.

The children were sent to bed around nine o'clock, to be called in time for Midnight Mass. When they were out of the way she'd set up the four or five card tables with chairs and centrepieces, then return to the stove for the final preparations. In just a few hours it would all come together according to her carefully premeditated plan. By the time the children were roused for their trip to the church the house was filled with the scent of cloves, emanating from the pan of rabbit broth on the top of the stove. More than anything else it was that smell which announced the arrival of the great event.

Margaret didn't go to church. Her Christmas duty was right there, in the kitchen. Her husband accompanied the children, and it was his responsibility to make sure all the guests were invited home after the service. By the time they got back everything was out. The table was full. There was rabbit pie; creamy, golden mustard pickles and chow; squares of cheese; slices of homemade bread an inch thick; the cakes from the cellar, now out of their tins and sliced and arranged decorously on special plates; a dish of divinity fudge; and the pies at the back, side by side, the droplets on the top of the lemon meringue catching the light like tiny Christmas ornaments.

When everyone came in she'd be standing by the stove, putting on the tea, looking like she was ready to burst. The guests, in an elevated state of Christmas goodwill, would remark how wonderful everything looked, and year after year she'd say it was nothing, a comment which belied the obvious aura of achievement and consummation which radiated from her. Some-one would say, "Margaret, you're a marvel!" and she would say "Go on now!" and tell them to help themselves.

She never sat down during the entire meal, not for a minute, just circulated continuously, replenishing the plates and teacups. "Would you like some more?" she would ask rhetorically as she deposited a second or third piece of rabbit pie on the half-empty plates. "Margaret, I couldn't eat another bite!" someone would protest, but if there was even the slightest hint of hesitation she would proceed undeterred. "Oh! have some more," she would say. "All we get in this life is a bite to eat."

From one year's end to the next there was nothing in her experience to match the way Margaret felt during the brief time when her family and friends were at their places, enjoying her creation. She moved among the tables with such flourish and aplomb that it seemed the entire meal might well have been scripted and choreographed. For those few moments Margaret was in her glory, vividly and triumphantly herself. It was a grand achievement, flawlessly performed and universally acclaimed within her small circle.

Late in the night, long after the last grateful guest had departed, and the children, taut with excitement, had finally dropped off to sleep, she finished cleaning up. It was time to fill the stockings and to start thinking about the goose, and the next day's meal, which always seemed to her an anticlimax. She was tired now, and the veins in her leg were aching. At three o'clock she sat down in the rocking chair beside the stove with a cup of tea and a piece of bread. The house was quiet, and she felt a great serenity in herself as she savoured the events of the past few hours. She glanced over at the table, now bare except for the tablecloth. It would stay there for one more meal, and then go back into the drawer, beside the ruffled curtains.

he register in the kitchen ceiling, above the stove, had always been one of his favourite spots in the entire house. It was his own special listening place. But one Christmas, when he was ten or eleven, he overheard something there which, fifty years later, could still bring back a feeling of sadness and bitter disappointment.

The register was a rectangular hole, about the size of a cookie pan, which allowed the warm air from the kitchen to move upstairs into the cold winter bedrooms. There was a grate in the register which was closed during the summer, when the upstairs rooms were already too hot from the sun on the roof. During the winter it was left open and, late in the evening, after he had been sent up to bed, there was light and heat which drifted up from below, along with the ebb and flow of grown-up conversation. It attracted him irresistibly. Many nights he would creep softly to the edge of the hole and listen to what was going on in the kitchen. The register became for him a small rend in the heavy curtain of secrecy and reserve which, in that society, separated children from the guarded world of adult experience.

If it was quiet in the kitchen it was almost impossible for him to get to the register without being heard. Many times he was chased back to his bed with a stern reprimand: "Jimmie, get away from that hole. Take those big ears of yours back to bed where they belong." But when there was noise below — laughter, or music, or loud conversation — he could get to the register undetected and settle down. It was his radio and late-night television combined. Some nights the dialogue was desultory and unremarkable, punctuated with long pauses. It wasn't really conversation, just an occasional, comfortable verbal touching between his parents. Other times there would be the confidential sharing of something that had happened during the day, and occasionally the sharp crackle of disagreement. If there was a ceilidh going on below he would sometimes take a blanket with him and sit, cross-legged, with it draped over his head, tent-fashion, so it covered both the register and himself. Other evenings he'd just lie there, and twice he fell asleep. Both times he woke up in the morning in his own bed.

He especially loved it when John Dan and Lena would visit. His own parents weren't much for telling stories, but John Dan was full of them. He was one of those people who seemed to remember everything he had ever seen or heard, and when he described an event which had taken place years before he could always recall what time of year it was, what day of the week it was, and what the weather was like. More than that, he had the ability to make everything sound interesting and important, as though the direction of the wind, or the condition of the roads on the day of his recounting, were matters of quintessential significance.

Jimmie learned many things listening at the register. He found out one night that his mother's brother in Charlottetown had borrowed some money from his father years before, and had never paid it back. He always knew his father had little use for his uncle Louis, but until that night had never known why. Another night he learned, to his amazement, that his father didn't believe everything the minister said. He also discovered that his parents worried a lot about money. Nothing ever came of it, but several times he heard his father say that he was thinking of going away in the wintertime so he could make enough money to pay off the note. He didn't know what a note was, but it was evident from his father's tone of voice that it was a serious matter.

One year, on Christmas Eve, Jimmie was stationed at his familiar listening post. His mother was preparing for the big dinner the next day, and the smell of her baking wafting up through the grate increased the sense of excitement and anticipation which had been building in him for days. His father, who had been to town that day, was seated at the table, removing the string from a brown package which, he could tell, had come from the store. Jimmie knew he shouldn't look, but the temptation was too great.

In the package was a miniature brush and comb set, with ivory on the handles. It was, obviously, a gift intended for his younger sister. "What did you get for Jimmie?" his mother queried. "Nothing," his father replied curtly. "He's old enough now that I don't think we need anything for him. Besides, there's just no money. Anyway, I think he knows the difference. The candy will be enough."

The disappointment was overwhelming. It was as though he had been struck a tremendous blow, and he felt hot tears well up in his eyes and run down his cheeks. It was all he could do to keep from sobbing out his grief. He lay there a while longer, hoping he would hear something to indicate his father had been joking. But nothing more was said, and he felt a fierce anger at his mother for not protesting the betrayal he felt. When she lifted the cover off the stove to add a stick to the fire he backed away from the register and retreated to his bed. The night was shattered, broken apart like a dropped dish, and it seemed that nothing so terrible had happened to him in his entire life.

He didn't go back to the register very often after that, and when he did it wasn't the same. The surreptitious delight of listening at the grate was greatly diminished, and though he didn't understand it at the time, years later he would come to the realization that his experience that Christmas Eve marked the beginning of his reluctant passage from one side of life's curtain to the other.

Charlie and the Paper Boy

He grew up poor, in a large family of brothers on the Miramichi. When he was old enough to work he became a lumberjack, and with his thick, tree-trunk of a body, and large powerful hands, he looked every inch the part. But as a young man he gave up the life of the woods for another vocation. He became an entertainer, and by the time his life was over his rich baritone voice, gregarious disposition and mischievous stage antics had established him as one of the country's best known and most beloved troubadours.

His name was Charlie Chamberlain, and during the 1950s and 1960s he became famous across the country as the lead male vocalist in the "down-east" band, "Don Messer and the Islanders." Charlie was always a show stopper. Whether at a one-night stand in some small Maritime community, on-stage in Hamilton or Calgary, or in front of the C.B.C. television cameras, he could take a song to the hearts of his audience in a way that was the envy of other performers. "He was a good-hearted, great fella," recalled an acquaintance, "and the sadder the song the better he liked it. He'd make himself cry, and make everyone else cry too."

Charlie was, perhaps more than anything else, a master of musical nostalgia. His sincere, even maudlin, renditions of traditional Irish folksongs, favourite hymns, or popular ballads were delivered with such unabashed sentimentality that his listeners felt somehow comforted and reassured. He touched them in deeply familiar places, and they loved him for it.

In 1953 Charlie and the rest of the band were living on the Island. Charlie had a house in Charlottetown, on Churchill Avenue, and on the afternoon of the day before Christmas he put in a call to his long-time friend, Russell Downe, inviting him to his place for a little talk and a few tunes. Russell was happy to oblige. He grabbed his guitar and went over, and before long the two men were seated on the edge of two chairs in the living room, one on either side of the Christmas tree, having their own little Christmas concert. They sang some carols, as well as other favourites, and were right in the middle of "Down in the Little Green Valley" when the doorbell rang.

It was a little fellow from up the street, the paper boy, who had come to collect his paper money. "Come on in," Charlie invited, and began to fumble in his pockets for the right change.

While this was happening the boy, wide-eyed, was staring at the tree. Charlie noticed his look of wonderment and asked, "Do you like my tree?"

"Yes sir," said the boy.

"Do you have a tree like that at your house?" Charlie asked off-handedly.

"No sir," was the soft, flat reply.

"You don't have a Christmas tree!" Charlie exclaimed incredulously.

"No."

"Do you have a turkey?"

"No."

"Any presents?"

"No."

By this point in the conversation, Charlie, guitar in hand, was looking quite disconcerted by the boy's replies.

"Why haven't you got anything for Christmas?" he queried.

"My father's not workin'. He told us we're gonna have Christmas next year," was the boy's answer.

"Do you have any brothers or sisters?"

"Yes."

"Well!" stated Charlie emphatically, "You must have a tree! That's all there is to it!"

With that he laid his guitar on the couch and walked over to the tree. His friend Russell watched in amazement as Charlie proceeded on a course of action that was so unexpected, and so impulsively generous, that after all these years it stands out vividly in his memory. "I will remember it as long as I live," he told me.

Charlie unplugged the Christmas tree lights, then reached through the branches and, with his big right hand, picked the tree off the floor — lights, ornaments, tinsel and all. Tree in hand, he marched out to the kitchen where a turkey was lying in the sink, the neck flopped out over the side. With his left hand he grabbed the turkey. "Open the door, Russell," he ordered, "we're going to make a little call."

"Show me where you live, young fella," he said, as he stepped outside, pulling the tree through the door behind him.

"It was quite a procession," recalled Russell. "The boy was ahead, and behind him came Charlie carrying the turkey and the tree, with the cord from the lights dragging in the snow. I was bringing up the rear, shaking my head in amazement, and laughing at the look of Charlie heading off up the street."

When they arrived at the paper boy's house his mother came out on the porch. "Open your door wide," shouted Charlie.

The woman, taken completely by surprise, blurted out, "Oh my Lord! Mr. Chamberlain! I don't believe it."

"Well, we're here anyway," retorted Charlie as he swooshed by her into the house. He proceeded to set the tree in a corner, and then strode out to the kitchen at the back of the house, where he deposited the massive Christmas bird in the sink.

"Merry Christmas," he called out, as he exited the house as abruptly and flamboyantly as he had entered.

As they walked back, Russell reminded Charlie that he now had neither tree nor turkey at his own place, and that the stores were closing in just a few minutes. "You're right, Russell," replied Charlie, a triumphant grin on his face. "I don't have a turkey and I don't have a tree. But I made someone happy. I've got that."

It was the kind of episode someone could write a song about — the kind of song Charlie Chamberlain would have loved to sing.

CHRISTMAS STOCKINGS

"I only had one pair of stockings to my name, so on Christmas Eve Day they'd be washed and dried by the stove so I'd have a clean stocking to hang up."

Albany

"When we'd put up our stocking we'd have the place picked out — where we were going to put the nail — oh months before that! And I'd have my nail, and the others would have theirs, and all those old stockings would be hangin' around. There'd be an orange and an apple, and the big thing that was so lovely was those great big raisins. Oh big! you don't see them now. The great big fellas. They'd be all wrapped in tissue paper. Goin' back upstairs, feeling those things in the stocking, Oh what a joy! Everything was so good!"

Melville

"Christmas Eve we always used to listen to a program on the radio. It had Little Nose and Santa in it . . . After that we figured it was time for bed, but we had to get the stockings first. In the kitchen . . . there was this big bottom drawer where all the big heavy wool work socks the men wore were kept. The fight would be on to try and get the biggest, fattest wool sock."

Dunstaffnage

"You'd hang up a sock if it wasn't so cold that you wouldn't take it off."

Springton

"We were lucky if we had a few goodies or a stick of candy in our stocking at Christmas. I thought one year that perhaps Santa might come back at New Year's if I hung up my stocking. All I got was a big potato."

Souris

The True Meaning of Crumbfest

This is the story of young Eckhart, a mouse. He had quick tiny feet, shiny black eyes and an extra-long tail. Eckhart lived with his family in a place called Rose Valley, Prince Edward Island.

It is also the story of a very great mystery; a mystery which all the mice in Rose Valley talked about, but which was never solved until the day Eckhart set off on his great adventure. It was the day he went boldly where no mouse had gone before, and discovered the true meaning of Crumbfest.

For Eckhart and the other mice, every year was divided into two parts: the Outside part, and the Inside part. During the long warm days they lived in a snug burrow beneath a spruce tree in the corner of a field, next to the woods. But when the days became shorter, and the great snows came, they left Outside and moved Inside, between the walls of the big white farmhouse where the people lived. The mice, of course, didn't refer to them as people. They called them "the straight ones," because of the way they walked.

Eckhart didn't like going Inside. None of the mice did. The narrow space between the walls, where they spent the winter, was a cold, dismal place. There was no grass there, or trees, or flowers; and no sunshine.

The Inside was also a hungry place. There was plenty of food in the house, but at night, the only time it was safe to go searching, it was almost always shut up in the little pantry off the kitchen — in jars, or in tins with tight covers. The only spot the mice could find food was on the kitchen floor, underneath the big wooden table where the people ate. There would usually be a few crumbs there, tiny bits of bread or biscuit which had tumbled down from above.

But there was one time of the year when all that changed.

Every year, in late December, just a few weeks after the mice had moved Inside, a most astonishing thing happened. Suddenly! as if by magic, there were crumbs everywhere. For several days the mice feasted, not just on bread or biscuit, but on cake, and cookies, and pie-crust.

The mice had a name for this time of abundance. They called it Crumbfest, and over the years it became the most important celebration in mouse society. "Merry Crumbfest," they would call out to one another as they scurried in and out of their hole in the wall, bringing back load after load of tasty morsels.

The young mice, like Eckhart, who had been born Outside during the summer, had only heard stories about Crumbfest, and so they looked forward to it with almost unbearable excitement. "Is it really as crumby as they say?" Eckhart asked his mother. "Oh yes, dear," she would answer, "it is the crumbiest time of the whole year."

Eckhart's grandfather, a skinny bent old mouse named Tomis, had lived longer than any of the other mice. He had celebrated three Crumbfests, and Eckhart asked him once why it happened every year. Old Tomis said he didn't know. He said it was a mystery. When Eckhart asked him a second time he twitched his tail in annoyance. "Don't ask so many questions," he said crossly. "Crumbfest happens, and that's all there is to it! Just be thankful, and don't waste your time trying to know things that mice can never know.

"I'm warning you, Master Eckhart," he added in a serious voice, "if you ask too many questions you may just ruin it for yourself and everyone else."

Eckhart felt puzzled and hurt. He didn't like to upset his grandfather, but he just wasn't satisfied with the old mouse's answer. Eckhart, you see, was a most curious creature. Indeed, his mother had told him once that his curiosity was just as long as his tail, and that one day it would get him into trouble.

The truth is, Eckhart had some doubts about Crumbfest. He thought maybe it was just a story the old mice had made up to help pass the time during the long, dark, Inside days. He once told his little sister, Mavis, that there was no such thing as Crumbfest, and she burst into tears. "Eckhart," she sobbed, "you are a hateful, horrid brother."

But then, one day, just when Eckhart was beginning to feel certain that he was right, the crumbs appeared.

It was amazing! Absolutely amazing!

The word spread quickly between the walls. "They've arrived! They've arrived!" everyone was saying. "The crumbs are here!"

Eckhart had never seen such excitement. Everyone was happy. Even Tomis, who hardly ever smiled, seemed to be in a good mood. And no one was more joyous than Eckhart. His dark little eyes were shining with delight as mouse after mouse came scampering back through the hole in the wall, cheeks bulging with delicious holiday goodies.

But all of that just made Eckhart even more curious. On the second day of Crumbfest, as he sat chewing on a big sticky raisin, he started thinking again about the reason for this most mysterious event. Right there and then he decided he must solve the riddle. He made up his mind to go exploring.

When he told some of the other mice about his intentions they looked at him in astonishment, and his friend Martin told him he was crazy. Everyone said it was just too dangerous.

When grandfather Tomis learned of Eckhart's plan he shook his head and said scoldingly, "You stubborn little scallywag, how long is it going to take you to learn your place in this world? I've told you over and over that mice are creatures of the Outside, and that we are not meant to know the secrets of the Inside. Besides, there's too much danger in it. It's too risky — far too risky!"

Old Tomis dropped his head and continued muttering in his whiskers. It seemed he had forgotten all about Eckhart, and was talking to himself. Without

75

saying a word, Eckhart left the old mouse. He scurried to the hole in the wall and out into the kitchen.

It was the middle of the night and the room was quite dark. But there was a moon Outside, and it shone through the windows, giving Eckhart just enough light to see where he was going.

It was also very quiet. Not a creature was stirring — except Eckhart.

He passed beneath the great wooden table. This was familiar territory, and he paused for a moment to decide where he would go from there. He looked across the room and saw a door leading into a hallway. Beyond that was the unknown, and, perhaps, the secret of Crumbfest. He knew that was where he must go.

As he passed through the doorway he could feel his heart pounding. He moved slowly at first, but then scampered across a mat and came to another door. He stopped and peered inside, twitching his nose, for he had become aware of a familiar scent in the air. In front of him was a wide room, with a shiny floor. There was a very large object near the door; something he had never seen before. He scampered underneath and poked his head out the other side.

And that's when he saw it!

Eckhart could scarcely believe his eyes. He looked again, but sure enough, it was still there.

It was a tree. A fir tree. A beautiful tree from the Outside was right there in front of him — on the Inside.

Eckhart ran over quickly and looked up into the branches. There, on the tree, were other things from the Outside. There was a long string of red berries — the kind that grow on the rose bushes along the fence — and some birds. They didn't look exactly like the birds he had seen Outside, but they were definitely birds, sitting very still in the branches.

It was all very surprising, and strange, and something told Eckhart that it must have something to do with Crumbfest, though he wasn't sure what.

There was a small table beside the tree and Eckhart ran quickly up one of the legs to get a better view. When he came up over the top there was another great surprise waiting for him. There, gathered together in a circle, were tiny animals from the Outside.

There were two cows, a horse with long ears and several sheep. There were also some tiny people there, and right in the middle a little box, with a baby sleeping in some straw. Eckhart walked over slowly and stood beside one of the sheep, which was just exactly the same size as he was. He remained there quietly for a few moments, standing just as still as the other animals.

And that's when it happened!

Eckhart felt something he had never felt before. It started somewhere inside of him, and spread out right to the very tips of all his whiskers, and to the end of his extra-long tail.

It wasn't exactly astonishment, and it wasn't exactly joy. It was wonder — that's what it was. Eckhart felt wonder-full.

It only lasted a short time, but Eckhart knew in that moment that he had discovered the meaning of Crumbfest. It came to him in a flash, and he knew his journey was over. It was now time to go back to the other mice and tell them his story.

He scampered down to the floor, and, with one last look at the tree, ran quickly —
    across the shiny floor,
    under the large object,
    out through the door,
    across the mat,
    through the other door,
    under the great table where the crumbs were,
    and into the hole in the corner.

When he arrived back between the walls the other mice could tell immediately that something sensational had happened. Eckhart had been away a half an hour — which is quite a long time for a mouse — and he looked different. Soon they were all gathered around him.

"Where have you been?" they asked. "What have you seen?" Even grandfather Tomis, looking especially interested, came close enough to hear.

Eckhart told them the story of his journey. He told them about the big room, the tree, the berries and the birds. And when he got to the part about the animals he lowered his head, straightened his tail, and said softly, "The mystery of Crumbfest is the mystery of the Outside and the Inside. When the Outside comes Inside it is a special time, for when the Outside and the Inside are together, Crumbfest happens."

For a moment no one spoke.

Most of the mice looked puzzled. And Tomis scowled. But there were a few whose eyes opened very wide, as though they had just heard a secret which they already knew.

In the years that followed, the story of Eckhart's adventure was passed down from generation to generation. The telling and retelling of the tale became an important part of the Crumbfest celebrations. Most of the mice still didn't go farther than the crumbs beneath the table, but there were a few who followed Eckhart's trail through the doorway. Like Eckhart they experienced for themselves the mystery of Crumbfest, and the wonder of a place where the Inside and the Outside are together.

CHRISTMAS STOCKINGS

"The worst thing to get would be that hard candy, because it would stick to the toe of your woollen stocking."

St. Peter's

"John Peter, Eugenie, Bernadette and their mother used to come to our place every Christmas Eve. [They were cousins, whose father had died.] John Peter would sleep with his mother, but the girls would all sleep together. Sometimes we would sleep five across the bed, because we couldn't stand to be separated. We'd hang up our stockings in the hall and we'd be up half the night to see if Santa Claus had come."

Wellington

"My most vivid memory of Christmas is the sight of fourteen stockings hung up side-by-side in the parlour on Christmas Eve."

Brockton

"Christmas Eve everyone was extra busy polishing and cleaning the house; preparing a box lunch for Santa Claus, which was carefully tied and placed on an outside shelf where the milk pails usually rested; and hanging socks near our stove or under the clock shelf."

Hampton

"I remember the long brown stockings hanging up by a thread. Mom would always thread a loop on the socks at the top and then you hung it over the back of a kitchen chair. You know there wouldn't be much in it because it wouldn't stand the pressure, with just this little thread holdin' it up."

Covehead Road

Maraks

t was Boxing Day, and a number of friends had dropped by for a visit. On the table in the kitchen was a plate piled high with bite-size pieces of broccoli, celery and carrots, and, alongside, a bowl filled to the brim with some kind of creamy garlic concoction for dipping. There was also a large platter of nachos, arranged artistically around a container of salsa, which had been blended together with processed cheese; and, beside that, some hoummos and pita bread. It wasn't exactly a traditional Island lunch; in fact, apart from the celery and carrots, there was nothing on the table that I had even tasted before the age of thirty-five.

But there was a surprise in the oven. It was something I'd been waiting all evening to share with my guests. When the moment seemed right I called everyone together and announced that I had a special treat for one and all. With affected aplomb I then placed on the counter before them a strange-looking type of food. It was something from the past, something as outdated and vestigial as homespun underwear or homemade lye soap, and all around the room, brows wrinkled in puzzlement. Their grandparents might have recognized it, but I was certain it would be as much a novelty to them as it had been to me. The looks on their faces told me I was right.

I cut it into thick slices and soon everyone was nibbling tentatively on the unexpected and unsolicited snack.

"Don't give me any," said one timorous soul, "I'll just help Allison with his."

"It's very fat," ventured another.

"What is this?" someone finally asked, giving me the perfect opportunity to tell my story. Over the years I had often heard the old people talk about "maraks," or "marakins," and many had said that in their memory they were as much a part of the Christmas menu as plum pudding, homemade doughnuts, meat pies or roast goose. Maraks, I learned, were a type of sausage made from the intestines of a cow, and because it was the practice on most farms to butcher an animal in December, when the weather became cold enough to hang the carcass in an outbuilding, the making and eating of maraks became a much anticipated part of the Christmas festivities.

I was curious to know more, and when it came to my attention that the Reverend Donald Nicholson, a retired clergyman, still made maraks every Christmas, I determined to go and see him. I was slightly apprehensive, fearing perhaps that this venerable churchman, from the old Presbyterian school of theological correctness, might consider sausages a frivolous topic, scarcely worthy of serious discussion. I also had it in my mind that it might be easy to offend such a person, and resolved to be on my guard against saying anything which might affront the old gentleman's entrenched sensibilities. I was, in other words, in a somewhat prejudiced state of mind.

Five days before Christmas I went for my visit. When I arrived at his door on the Meadow-bank Road at nine o'clock in the morning, he welcomed me congenially, shook my hand firmly, and invited me inside. As I bent over in the porch to take off my boots, he surprised me by speaking a few phrases in Gaelic. He informed me that he had just asked me to take off my coat and make myself at home. It seemed an auspicious beginning. Immediately I became more relaxed, and began to feel that it might be an interesting morning. I was not disappointed.

He led me into his living room which was dominated by an enormous grandfather clock. It was a handsome piece, more than six feet tall, with a very large brass pendulum, the size of a lunch plate. The clock, which seemed a third presence in the room, marked off the hours and the halves, and as we spoke it seemed entirely appropriate that our conversation, about a social order now largely disappeared, should have been measured so precisely by the solemn chiming. The clock in one corner, and the dignified old man in the other, seated straight in his chair with his arms folded across his chest, was a powerfully evocative picture. I felt deeply in that moment the relentless march of change, and the poignant struggle of the older generation to maintain its fidelity to a time which had been so thoroughly overrun by the hard trample of modernity.

My host, a remarkably robust eighty-seven years old, was born and raised in Hartsville, which, in earlier days, was referred to locally as "the Scotch Settlement." He told me that during his boyhood there were a number of people living in the community who had been born in the Old Country. They had become Prince Edward Islanders, but their customs and manners remained thoroughly Scottish. Many of them continued to speak the old language, and, in recollecting those early years, Donald informed me that Gaelic was the currency of daily conversation in his own home. The practice began to erode during his childhood, but he said that he had an older brother who scarcely knew a word of English until he started school. Apparently the boy's grandfather, who lived with them, insisted on Gaelic immersion for the grandchildren. "They will pick up the English soon enough," was his stalwart opinion.

When I asked Donald if he was able to speak the old language, he confessed that he had lost much of it, but hastened to add that for his private devotions he read every day from his Gaelic Bible, which was lying open on the table next to his chair. It occurred to me that I was probably sitting across from the last of his kind in the entire province, and marvelled that there could have been so much change in one lifetime. I thought to myself that even his prescient old Scottish grandfather would have been shocked had he been able to anticipate the cultural transformation that would occur during the lifetime of his grandsons. They did, indeed, "get the English soon enough" — and much more.

It took me some time to raise the topic of the maraks, even though I had broached the question on the telephone before my visit. I knew enough about older Islanders to realize that any undue haste or impatience in getting to the point might be considered unseemly, even discourteous. I had learned from them that a conversation, like a winding stream, has its own natural flow, and that any abrupt forcing of the discussion would be resisted instinctively as an impropriety. I had also learned that a direct approach when attempting to solicit information, or anything else, from members of that older generation could sometimes trigger a strong retentive reflex. In my experience some of them could take a perverse delight in withholding anything which was requested in an overly eager fashion. This, happily, was not the case with the Reverend Nicholson, and when I eventually negotiated the topic of the maraks into the conversation he seemed pleased to answer my questions.

He acknowledged that maraks, or "mealy puddings," were common Christmastime fare in Hartsville during his boyhood, and that he had kept alive the tradition of making them every year. "As a matter of fact," he said, "we made some here yesterday, and before you go we'll go out to the kitchen and you can have a look at them.

"I had some before I went to bed last night," he confided. "In fact, I had quite a feed. It's a wonder I even woke up this morning. They're quite strong you know."

When I asked him how they were made he became very methodical in his responses. He said that first of all the intestine of the butchered animal was cut into appropriate lengths, turned inside out, and cleaned thoroughly. Next the pieces were placed in a solution of salt and soda, and left to soak overnight. The following morning they were stuffed with a mixture of oatmeal, onions, suet, salt and pepper — ingredients as basic and unpretentious as the people themselves. They were then tied at the ends with a string, leaving enough room for the stuffing to expand inside the intestinal casing during the cooking. Finally, the maraks were placed in a large pot of boiling water. He told me that early in the boiling each of them had to be pricked in several places with a needle. Speaking as a man with firsthand experience he then cautioned, "If you don't prick them they'll go to the ceiling."

The boiling of the maraks took from two to three hours, after which they were ready to eat. "I like them steaming, right out of the pot," he said, "but most people I know prefer to let them cool, and then slice them up and fry them in a bit of butter, or heat them in the oven, until the juice starts to flow. There's a lot of fat in them," he admitted, "and some people today probably wouldn't eat them because of the cholesterol. But I am eighty-seven and I've been eating them all my life.

"I also like heavy cream on my porridge," he added with a smile.

During our conversation Donald became most animated, and most engaging, when he informed me that his two grandsons, Roger and Allan MacPhee, had spent much of the previous day in his kitchen, preparing maraks under his watchful supervision. "But they did the whole thing themselves," he reported proudly.

It obviously pleased him immensely that the young men were interested in learning to make maraks while he was alive to teach them, and that after his death they will be able to carry on a tradition which will connect them, not only with their grandfather, but with a Christmas tradition leading all the way back to the old Scottish community in Hartsville, and, beyond that, to Scotland itself. He agreed quickly when I suggested that the stuffing and boiling of the maraks was more than a culinary art, but had became an important ritual of family continuity. "Yes," he said emphatically, "that's it."

Before I left, Donald took me out to the kitchen to see the maraks, and it is no exaggeration to say they seemed the most unattractive food I had ever witnessed. They looked like . . . well . . . like intestines — darkened and distended by the boiling. I don't know what I was expecting, but was somewhat taken aback by the sight of them. "Mmmm," I said softly, disguising my surprise, "so these are maraks."

I could imagine them hanging behind the wood stove in a farm kitchen of ninety or a hundred years ago; but there, beside the stainless steel sink in Donald's modern kitchen, they seemed strikingly out of place. They were just too earthy; too unprocessed; too close to the blood and guts of things.

But I will never forget the look of them.

In this year, 1993, the sights and smells of Christmas are on every hand, but I'm certain that none will endure in my memory as long as the homely sight of that roaster pan filled with maraks sitting on that old Scot's kitchen counter; or the savoury smell of suet, oatmeal and onions as he cut through one of them and presented me with a large piece. It was a kind gesture, and as it passed from his hand to mine I felt a very great affection for this elderly man in his grey, buttoned sweater. I realized I was receiving much more than a piece of mealy pudding. He was sharing himself, and the consecrated memory of his people before him, and I experienced in that moment the deep pleasure of Christmas communion.

As I was leaving I thanked him for his co-operation and complimented him on his obvious fitness. I was extremely pleased with the morning, and that I had managed to avoid any of the conversational potholes I had feared before the visit. Then, as I was pulling on my boots, I asked him if he was still driving his car. It seemed a harmless bit of small talk. He said he was, and then added wryly that he only feels old when someone asks him if he is still driving. "Damn," I thought to myself; and though I didn't try to repair the moment, I regretted very much having opened my mouth, fearing my inane comment had probably insulted his crusty Scottish pride. But he shook my hand warmly as I left, and wished me a happy Christmas.

As I walked across the yard I thought of the grandfather clock. Deep in the house it would soon be striking twelve.

Alias, Santa

Is there a Santa Claus?
Of course there is.
Like Tennyson's brook
he will go on forever.

J. Austin Trainor

Ahhh, Santa Claus!

Old and wise without a trace of adult cynicism, jolly and exuberant with out affectation, kind and generous without seeking recompense, busy and competent while in a state of perpetual serenity — he is one of the great creations of Northern European civilization.

And, in addition to all of that, he flies.

Santa is the great mythic figure of childhood imagination, and belief in him a cornerstone of childhood cosmology; and it would be no exaggeration to say that, in our culture, there is no moment which marks so clearly the termination of childhood innocence as the day a girl or boy is forced to come to terms with the awful truth of Santa's alleged non-existence. It is one of the most fundamental shifts in perception we ever experience; or, as one Island man put it, " . . . the responsibilities of life really began when Santa didn't come down the chimney anymore."

A woman from O'Leary remembered bitterly the traumatic time when her belief was cruelly shattered by an older sibling. "I was about eight when I found out," she said, "and cried for what seemed a week." She explained that her brother told her in a fit of rage. "He had just received a tanning for something I had done. He never told on me, but his way of getting back and venting his anger was telling me the terrible secret about Santa Claus." Another woman, from the North Shore, recalled that "belief in Santa didn't last long at our place." She was one of many children, and stated that the older brothers and sisters "couldn't bear to see you still believin'."

It is not surprising that youngsters hold on to their belief in Santa for as long as they can, and that most parents play their part in fostering and prolonging faith in this patron saint of childhood enchantment. A man who grew up in Bangor, Prince Edward Island, recalled the time in his boyhood when he was beginning to entertain early doubts about the "reality" of Santa Claus. Christmas morning his father took him outside and drew his attention to the reindeer droppings scattered on the snow on the barn roof. He noted that they looked very much like horse droppings, but said he was eager to accept his father's explanation for the phenomenon. It helped keep the belief alive for at least another year.

Another Islander, now an old woman, recalled that her belief was confirmed year after year by the long grey hairs from Santa's beard which could be found every Christmas morning near the hung stockings. There was an old mare in the barn with a gray mane, but she said it never occurred to her at the time to imagine that the stray hairs were anything else but Santa's errant whiskers. Like most children, she resisted doubt, the way a city resists invasion.

Another woman, who grew up on St. Peter's Island, reported that her belief in Santa Claus was supported by a custom that may have been unique to that little off-shore community. For most children the surest sign of Santa's mysterious visitation was the small deposit of goodies in the toe of their stockings. But not on St. Peter's Island. The children there were informed on Christmas morning that Santa had come and gone, and that they should go looking in the seaweed for the treats he had left. "We used to have seaweed all around the house for banking," said my informant, "and we'd go out and dig in the seaweed, and we'd run into some apples, and then we'd run into the house, and then we'd go back out and find some oranges, and then long canes of candy all in amongst the seaweed in around the house." She said it was "impossible not to believe" that those hidden treasures had been placed there by Santa.

A child's belief in Santa Claus did not require visual verification. You didn't have to see him to believe in him. Indeed, the wonderful dread of actually encountering Santa could inculcate a degree of excitement bordering on discombobulation. "When Santa Claus would come to the concert at our school my heart would jump right up in my throat and stay there the whole time he was there," was how one woman from Monticello described the experience.

Like this woman, most children growing up on Prince Edward Island before mid-century were most liable to have their close encounter with Santa at the annual Christmas Concert in the little one-room schoolhouse. Others, however, would get to see him at one of the larger stores, and of all the Santas in all the stores, there was none who sat more children on his knee, or was better remembered, than the Santa at Holman's in Charlottetown. Holman's was the store "where old friends meet," and, for many Island youngsters it was the place of their first memorable meeting with their old friend Santa. "He was wonderful-perfect," was how one Charlottetown woman described him.

The man behind the beard at Holman's was a Charlottetown resident, J. Austin Trainor, and in the minds of many Islanders, "Austin Trainor was Santa Claus." It was amusing to hear the recollection of one man whose parents took him every Christmas to Holman's to see Santa. He said that one year his aunt from Wilmot was visiting their home and took him to visit the Santa at Woolworth's. Apparently, after listing off the toys he wanted, he added, "I know you're not Santa, so you be sure and tell the real Santa at Holman's what I want."

In discussing with a number of Islanders their memories of Austie Trainor — alias Santa Claus — I discovered some of the reasons for the great success of his annual performance. His deep, resonant, musical voice was mentioned by everyone, and one woman said that he had the perfect shape for the role. "He was so round he was square," was her ingenious description of the man. Another woman, a relative, said he had an "incredible sense of presence," which he had developed as a young man during the several years he spent on the vaudeville circuit in the Boston area.

Again and again I have been surprised by how vividly, and how fondly, Trainor is recalled by many Islanders. I was talking on the street one day with Rollie MacKinnon, and asked him if he remembered him. "Well I guess I do," he said, and his face lit up immediately, as though someone had just plugged in the tree lights. He then began to mimic Trainor's sonourous voice, and I doubled over in delight as he recited, word for word, the familiar monologue which opened each of Austie's radio performances.

Another Charlottetown woman reflected that the reason "Austie" was so perfect for the part was the utter sincerity of his feeling for children, and the great respect he had for their belief in Santa Claus. She said that playing the part was much more than a job for him; rather, it was "like a sacred vocation." He spent a lot of time "making-up," and, according to a family member, he was so serious about getting into the role that even when he played the part on the CFCY radio program, "The Sleepy Town Express," he always wore his entire outfit, including the same clean white gloves he wore at the store. Trainor's close identification with Santa was expressed in three stanzas from a long Christmas poem he composed, in which he imagined himself flying an airplane over the Island on Christmas Eve.

> My eyes how they twinkle, my dimples how merry,
> as I cross o'er the Strait above the car ferry,
> and the beard on my chin is as white as the snow,
> as I throttle my motor above New Glasgow.

Tomorrow there'll be such a great lot of fun,
for the kiddies, think I, when I'm o'er Kensington.
There'll be toys for the kids, and a doll for each lass,
in Bonshaw, Miscouche, Kelly's Cross and Dundas.

An airplane for Johnnie, a paint book for Sally,
in Newcastle, Milton, Mt. Stewart, and Tyne Valley.
There are many such places, I can't say them all,
but all may be sure that old Santa will call.

Mickey Place worked at CFCY during the time that Austie was the "radio-Santa," and was most eloquent in describing the man's enduring legacy. He said that "every Santa Claus on Prince Edward Island since Austie Trainor has always been Austie to some extent," and that, in his opinion, "No other place in the world has quite the same kind of Santa Clauses as we have in Prince Edward Island, and that's because of Austie." The point might seem over-stated, but it is, at the very least, a tribute to the memory of a man who interpreted the legend of Santa Claus with such consummate skill for an entire generation of Islanders.

Catherine Hennessey, a friend of the Trainor family, said that Austie was wonderfully pro-tective of the children's belief in Santa. When I told her I was going to write about him, but that I was concerned about publishing a story which might inadvertently undermine even one child's belief in Santa, she replied immediately, "That's what Austie would have cared about the most. He would have wanted to protect the children."

Perhaps the best example of this fidelity on the part of Austie Trainor comes from the memory of Patsy Sinclair Faulkner. When she was a little girl she was, like so many other children, taken to Holman's for a visit with Santa. She sat on his knee, felt the brush of his whiskers on her cheek, and told him her heart's desire. There was no doubt in her mind that she had spoken to Santa. It was many years later she discovered that the wonderful man was J. Austin Trainor, her grandfather.

emory is a great enigma. How is it that after fifty, sixty, or even seventy years entire periods of a person's life can be forgotten almost entirely, while other experiences survive, undiminished by the passage of time, and remain as luminous and intact as if they had happened just yesterday?

It is that way with Christmas memories. Old men and women often express frustration over their inability to remember clearly the circumstances of their childhood Christmases; and yet, almost invariably, there is at least one memory which stands out clearly amid the blur of forgetfulness. They often can recall that one defining experience, a memory so indelibly vivid that after half a century or more it can be recalled with ease. Whether pleasant, or grievous, it takes them back to a time long ago when they looked at the world through a child's eyes, and experienced Christmas with a child's heart. For reasons which I do not understand, that preserved memory has become for them a touchstone of Christmas experience; and often, in relating the experience to me, they have concluded with the revealing little phrase — "and that was Christmas!"

One man's greatest fascination, and point of reference, was the Christmas tree. He said that once the tree went up, a day or two before Christmas, he would often pull on his boots and go outside the house for the sheer pleasure of coming back in, to experience it afresh. Another Islander also recalled the tree as being at the heart of her Christmas experience, but for her it was getting the tree that was the biggest thrill. She and her brother would go to the woods and cut down a tree and then "stand in the yard, frozen yet proud," and display it. They would wait for their mother to come to the door and inspect their selection. "If she liked it, we kept it, and if she didn't, it was back to the woods," she added.

For other Islanders it is the memory of food which is etched most deeply in their remembrance. One elderly Island woman, when asked to relate her most outstanding Christmas memory, responded immediately, "a goose and a duck and a fire in the parlour." Some of the memories of Christmas food are rather general, but others are wonderfully precise. One woman remembered with obvious relish the "saltpork, pickles and beets," after Midnight Mass, and another a "white cake with walnuts on the top." According to a person who grew up in Fox-

ley River, the Christmas menu at their place included ". . . roast goose, plum loaf, cheese, cold boiled pork, pickles, grapes, decorated cookies, and, everyone's favourite, Danny Boy peanut butter."

Then there were the Christmas doughnuts, which are mentioned again and again in the recollections of older Islanders. One man recalled the Christmas Eve ritual of his mother deep-frying doughnuts in the pork-fat from the recently butchered pig. He described in detail the sight and sound of the doughnuts sizzling on the top of the stove, and how his mother would shake the fat off each of them before placing them on the kitchen table. It amazes me that the sight of a doughnut could be recollected with such accuracy; and how, after all these years, the full intensity of a boy's Christmas emotions is connected to that single moment in time.

In the mind of another Island man the most deeply etched Christmas memory is that of his grandmother's home-made spruce beer. He confessed, "My memories of this ritual are scarce" but said that one thing did stand out in his mind. "I remember," he said, "that before Granny would serve any of the beer she would take the poker from the stove and stick the top into the fire until it was red hot. She would then stick the top of the poker into the beer to make it sizzle and give it more kick." I wondered, as he spoke, whether his grandmother actually possessed some age-old wisdom about the effects of thrusting the hot poker in the brew, or whether it was just another example of the natural theatricality of that folk culture.

In recounting her earliest memories of Christmas, Maud MacDonald from Monticello recalled with obvious delight the special edition of the *Family Herald* which came at Christmas. She told me that throughout the years there were never any coloured illustrations in the paper, but at Christmas it would be "all red and green." "I remember waiting for that special holiday edition," she said, "and while it might seem like a small thing, at the time it was a very big thrill."

A woman from O'Leary said that what she remembers best was the custom of putting a lighted lamp in the window early Christmas morning. She said it was a signal to her cousins across the field that everyone was up at her place. Her cousins did the same, and when she saw the lamp shining she would walk across the field in the pre-dawn darkness, guided by the beckoning glow of the lamp in their window. "Today," she said, "I miss those early treks across the field to see my cousins' gifts on Christmas morning."

The pleasure of congenial adult company is a precious thing to children, and for some Islanders the Christmases of their childhood are forever associated with events in the community when everyone was drawn together in the jovial spirit of holiday goodwill. Christmas, it seemed, had the power to transform parents and other big people into children.

One man from Kelly's Cross recalled that on the afternoon of Christmas Day, all the community would gather on the steep road by the church and go coasting. For that brief time the stern preoccupations of adult responsibility were banished, and everyone was joined together — literally — in the simple fun of sliding down the hill together. "Adults as well as children would bring their sleds up the hill," he recalled, "and when they would get to the top they would hook up twenty or thirty sleighs together. When all the sleighs were attached they would all pile on and go down the hill."

Another Islander, from St. George's, remembered the community groundspruce excursions which took place during his boyhood. He said that "gangs of girls and boys, men and women, would comb the woodland," collecting the groundspruce, and that just before Christmas they would all gather at someone's house and have a frolic. "It was a real party," he remembered fondly, "with music, and dancing, and, of course, food." The long strands of running spruce were taken out of the sacks and "strung into garlands, and entwined into wreaths, which would then be used to decorate the church."

Not all the memories of Christmas are pleasant. One man said that his house smelled "nice" at Christmas, but that by the time they all sat down to the Christmas dinner his mother would be so tired from all the preparing that she wouldn't be able to eat. "I can still remember her being so exhausted," he recalled, "that there would be tears in her eyes."

In another household the father had died during the previous year, and at Christmas the mother was so ill she was barely able to get out of her bed. There were ten children in the home, and one of the surviving daughters remembers that "the only thing my mother could come up with that year was some raisin bread." She said they always had raisin bread at Christmas, but that year, "it was the main and only course."

Some Islanders recall with great clarity the figures of Christmas past. One woman told me that her best and clearest Christmas memory is the sight of her father at the bedroom door in the semi-darkness of Christmas morning, the barn lantern in his hand, telling her it was finally time to get up and go downstairs. "He was like an angel," she said. Another man remembered the look of his father, standing in the front of the box-sleigh with the reins in his hands, as they drove to Midnight Mass in Vernon River. That sight has become forever locked in his memory. "I remember feelin' all warm and safe under his guidance," he concluded.

Whereas some older men and women are unable to recall a single one of the presents they received in recent years, many are able to picture, with photographic clarity, a special gift they received as a child. It might have been as simple as a little red shovel, a miniature straw broom, a revolving wooden noise-maker, a toy horse on a wheeled platform, a set of five pencils with their name printed in gold letters on the side, or a cheap harmonica, and the strong, lingering, metallic taste which resulted from attempting to play it. On the other hand, some gifts are remembered because they so exceeded expectations that the recipients could scarcely believe they were for them.

One woman was able to remember clearly the appearance of a doll she received from her older brother, Alfred, who was overseas during the First World War. He sent the money home, and his mother bought the doll and put it under the tree for her. She said it was made of that "plastic-like material which you could break easily," probably porcelain; and that "its arms and legs were hollow in the bottom and stuffed on top." She also recalled that it had "a little blue coat with a fleece-trimmed hood," as well as "white muffs and white overshoes"; and that she kept it wrapped in a blanket so it wouldn't get dirty. Her father made a crib for it, and Santa also brought her a small gray suitcase for the doll's clothes. "It was made of hard-pressed paper," she said, "and had a little handle on it," and as she spoke it was possible to picture it exactly. Her brother Alfred never came home. "He was killed overseas," she related sadly, "and I guess that is the reason I treasured the doll for years, and then gave it to my first child. It was a long time ago, but I will never forget that doll, and the memories that go with it."

My own defining Christmas memory from childhood is of an ornament: a tiny metal blue bell, about two inches high. There was nothing extraordinary about it, and as far as I can remember it didn't even have a clapper, but that mute little "Jesus-bell" spoke to me resoundingly of angels in the clouds, shepherds on the ancient hills, snow falling softly around the streetlight in front of our house on Willow Avenue, the intimate, whispering tryst of anticipation I shared with my sister Leona, the once-a-year treat of my mother's mince tarts, and the fizz up my nose on Christmas Eve of Canada Dry ginger ale. When it came out of the box every Christmas and was hung in the branches that little bell was a token of all the Christmas sweetness I had ever experienced.

Oh yes! That was Christmas!

David Weale teaches history at the University of Prince Edward Island. He is the author of the bestselling book *Them Times*, as well as a number of other books and articles on the history and folk culture of Prince Edward Island. He has a daughter and four sons; Joey, age 13, is the youngest, and he loves to draw.

A native of Prince Edward Island, Dale McNevin started drawing seriously in 1990. She has since illustrated two books and has had numerous showings of her work around the Island.